Graham Travers

Mona Maclean, medical student

A novel

Graham Travers

Mona Maclean, medical student
A novel

ISBN/EAN: 9783744640367

Printed in Europe, USA, Canada, Australia, Japan

Cover: Foto ©Andreas Hilbeck / pixelio.de

More available books at **www.hansebooks.com**

MONA MACLEAN

MEDICAL STUDENT

A NOVEL

BY

GRAHAM TRAVERS

IN THREE VOLUMES

VOL. II.

WILLIAM BLACKWOOD AND SONS
EDINBURGH AND LONDON
MDCCCXCII

CONTENTS OF THE SECOND VOLUME.

CHAP.   PAGE

XX. ST RULES, ... 1

XXI. THE FLYING SCOTSMAN, . . . 12

XXII. DR ALICE BATESON, ... 35

XXIII. A RENCONTRE, ... 45

XXIV. A CLINICAL REPORT, . . . 65

XXV. A VOICE IN THE FOG, . . 74

XXVI. A CHAT BY THE FIRE, . . 86

XXVII. A NEOPHYTE, ... 95

XXVIII. THE COLONEL'S YARN, . . 117

XXIX. "YONDER SHINING LIGHT," . 136

XXX. MR STUART'S TROUBLES, . . 147

XXXI. STRADIVARIUS, ... 159

XXXII. CHUMS, ... 177

XXXIII. CARBOLIC! . . . 185

XXXIV. PALM-TREES AND PINES, . 196

XXXV. WEEPING AND LAUGHTER, . . 214

XXXVI. NORTHERN MISTS, . . 230

XXXVII. THE ALGÆ AND FUNGI, . . 241

XXXVIII. THE BAZAAR, ... 254

XXXIX. THE BALL, ... 272

MONA MACLEAN,

MEDICAL STUDENT.

———◆———

CHAPTER XX.

ST RULES.

WHEN Mona appeared at the breakfast-table next morning, Rachel regarded her with critical dissatisfaction.

"I wonder you don't get tired of that dress," she said, as she poured out the tea—from the *brown* teapot. "It's very nice of course, and as good as new, but changes are lightsome, and one would think you would sometimes prefer to wear something more youthful-like. Pity your print's at the wash."

Mona looked out of the window.

"I have another," she said, "if you think it won't rain."

"Oh no. And besides, you can take your waterproof."

"It's not so much that I mind getting anything spoiled, as that I hate to be dressed unsuitably; but I do think it is going to be a beautiful day."

She left the room as soon as she had finished breakfast, and returned in about ten minutes.

"A gavotte in cream and gold," she said, making a low curtsey. "I hope it meets with your approval."

"My word!" said Rachel, "you do look the lady! and it's cheap stuff too. Why, I declare you would pass for a beauty if you took the trouble to dress well. It's wonderful how you become that hat!"

"Took a little trouble to dress well!" ejaculated Mona, mentally. "A nice thing to say to a woman who makes dress her first aim in life!"

They walked in to Kirkstoun, and there took the coach. Mona would fain have gone outside, but Rachel wanted to point out the lions they passed on the way, and she considered that they got their "penny's worth" better inside. Fortunately there were not many passengers, and Mona succeeded in placing herself on the windward side of two fishwives.

About noon they reached St Rules, and wandered rather aimlessly about the streets, paying incidental visits to the various places of note. Rachel had about as much idea of acting the part of *cicerone* as she had of trimming hats, or making scones, or keeping shop, or indeed of doing anything useful; and she was in a constant state of nervous perturbation, lest some officious guide should force his services upon them, and then expect a gratuity.

The season was over and the visitors were few, so Mona's pretty gown attracted not a little attention. Simple as it was, she regretted fifty times that she had put it on; Rachel's dress would have escaped notice but for the contrast between them.

It was positively a welcome interlude when they arrived at the pastry-cook's; but at the door Rachel stood aside obsequiously, to give place to a lady who came up behind them "in her carriage," and then gave her own order in a shamefaced undertone, as if she had no right to make use of the shop at the same moment as so distinguished a personage. Poor Mona! She thought once more of Lady Munro, and she sighed.

"The only other thing that we really need to see," said Rachel, wiping her hands on a crumpled paper bag that happened to lie beside her, "is the Castle. I'll be glad to rest my legs a bit, while you run round and look about you."

She had at least shown her good sense in reserving the Castle as a *bonne bouche*. Mona's irritation vanished as she stood in the enclosure and saw the velvety green turf under foot, the broad blue sky overhead, the bold outline of ruined masonry round about, and the "white horses" riding in on the rugged coast below. She was wandering hither and thither, examining every nook and cranny, when suddenly, in an out-of-the-way corner she came upon a young man and a girl in earnest conversation. The girl started and turned her back, and Mona left them in peace.

"Surely I have seen that face before," she thought, "and not very long ago. I know! It

is that silly little minx, Matilda Cookson. I
hope the young man is up to no mischief."

In another moment the "silly little minx"
was swept out of her mind; for, standing on a
grassy knoll, laughing and talking with Rachel,
she saw Dr Dudley.

An instinctive rush of surprise and pleasure,
a feeling of uneasiness at the thought of what
Rachel might be saying, a sense of satisfaction
in her own fresh girlish gown,—all these passed
through Mona's mind, as she crossed the open
space in the sunshine.

"Well," said Dudley, as she joined them,
"this can give a point or two even to Castle
Maclean."

"Do you think so?" she responded, gravely.
"That is high praise."

He laughed. "Have you seen that gruesome
dungeon?"

"Not properly. I am on my way to it now."

He turned to walk with her, and they leant
over the railing looking down on the blackness
below. A few feet from the top of the dungeon
a magnificent hart's-tongue fern sprang from a
crevice, and curled its delicate, pale-green fronds
over the dank, dark stone.

"How lovely!" said Mona.

"Yes," he said. "And it is not only the force of contrast. Its gloomy surroundings really do make it more beautiful."

"Yes," said Mona, relentlessly; "but it is not what Nature meant it to be."

"True," he replied. "Yet who would wish it transplanted!"

Presently he turned away, and looked over the rough blue sea.

"This place depresses me unspeakably," he said. "It reminds me of a book of 'martyr stories' I had when I was a child. I have a mental picture now of a family sitting round a blazing fire, and saying in awestruck whispers, 'It's no' sae cheery as this the nicht i' the sea tower by St Rules.' What appalling ideas of history they give us when we are children!" And he added half absently—

> " ' Sitzt das kleine Menschenkind
> An dem Ocean der Zeit,
> Schöpft mit seiner kleinen Hand
> Tropfen aus der Ewigkeit.' "

Mona looked up with sparkling eyes and made answer—

" ' Schöpfte nicht das kleine Menschenkind
   Tropfen aus dem Ocean der Zeit,
Was geschieht verwehte wie der Wind
   In den Abgrund oder Ewigkeit.' "

"Go on, go on," she said, regardless of his
unconcealed surprise, "the best thought comes
last." So he took up the strain again :—

" ' Tropfen aus dem Ocean der Zeit
   Schöpft das Menschenkind mit kleiner Hand.
Spiegelt doch, dem Lichte zugewandt,
   Sich darin die ganze Ewigkeit.' "

"I don't know," he said, moodily. "There
was precious little of Eternity in the drops that
were doled out to me."

"Not then," said Mona; "but when you were
old enough to turn them to the light, you could
see the eternal even there."

His face relaxed into a smile. This girl was
like an outlying part of his own mind.

They strolled slowly back to Rachel.

"Do you enjoy sight-seeing?" he asked.

"The question is too big. Cut it down."

"Nay, I will judge for myself,—if you are
not too tired to turn back to the town."

"Not a bit."

When Rachel heard of the proposal, she rose

to her feet, with considerable help from Mona and from a stout umbrella. She would fain have "rested her legs" a little longer, and the necessity of acting the part of chaperon never so much as crossed her mind; but the honour of Dr Dudley's escort through the streets of St Rules was not to be lightly foregone.

The first half-hour brought considerably more pain than pleasure to Mona. She was straining every nerve to draw out the best side of Rachel; and this, under the circumstances, was no easy task.

Rachel's manner was often simple, natural, and even admirable, when she was speaking to her inferiors; but the society of any one whom she chose to consider her superior was sure to draw out her innate vulgarity. Mona understood Dr Dudley well enough to know that he had no regal disregard for what are known as "appearances," and she suffered more for him than for herself.

It did not occur to her that Rachel was acting very effectively the part of the damp, black wall, which was throwing the dainty fern into more brilliant relief.

"It is all his own doing," she thought, indignantly. " Why has he brought this upon himself and me? And it will fall upon me to keep Rachel from talking about it for the next week."

Fortunately, though Rachel trudged about gallantly to the last, she soon became too tired to talk, and then Mona gave herself up to the enjoyment of the hour. Either Dr Dudley knew St Rules by heart, or he possessed a magnetic power of alighting on the things that were worth seeing. Curious manuscripts and half-effaced inscriptions; stained-glass windows and fine bits of carving; forgotten paintings, and quaint old vergers and janitors who had become a part of the buildings in which they had grown old;—all served in turn as the text for his brilliant talk. He might well say that talking was his *Verderben.*

Finally they wandered again through the ruins of the cathedral.

" 'Pull down the nests and the rooks will fly away!'" quoted Dudley, rather bitterly. " Here at least we have the other side of the ' martyr stories.' "

" I think sight-seeing is simply delightful," said Mona, as he stowed them into the coach; " but one wants special eyes to do it with."

" Everything becomes more interesting when seen 'through a temperament,' " he said. " I am glad if mine has served as a makeshift."

" She won't spot *that* reference," he thought to himself.

That evening all three made reflections about the day's outing.

" It came off wonderfully well, considering that I went in search of it," thought Dudley. " I fully expected it to be a dead failure. She *must* have met the draper accidentally."

" He is very gentlemanly and amazingly clever," thought Rachel ; " and he seemed as pleased at the meeting as any of us. But how my legs *do* ache !"

" I'll no more of this masquerading !" thought Mona. " I will take the first opportunity of asking Rachel's permission to tell him the whole truth. Perhaps he will take it all as a matter of course."

But when she went up to dinner the next day, Rachel calmly informed her that Dr Dudley had gone. " He has just walked up to the station with a bag in his hand," she said, " and Bill had a lot of luggage on a hurley. I think it's a queer sort of thing that he didn't look in

and say good-bye, after we were all so friendly-
like yesterday."

Mona smiled a little drearily.

" He might well say ' so long,' " she said to
herself, an hour later, as she sat on the battlements of Castle Maclean. " Looked at in the
abstract, as a period of time, three months is a
pretty fair sample of the commodity ! "

Thus does the feminine mind, while striving
to grasp the abstract, fall back inevitably into
the concrete !

" As a man," said Mona, " he is not a patch
upon the Sahib ; but I never had such a playfellow in my life ! "

CHAPTER XXI.

THE FLYING SCOTSMAN.

"What do you think, my dear?" said Rachel, a few days later, with beaming face. "I have just had a letter from my niece. Would you like to hear it?"

"Very much," said Mona. "'First Impressions of a New Continent.' Is it the first you have had?"

"No, it's the second. She's no great hand at the letter-writing. But there's more 'impressions' in this. She says the difficulty of getting servants is beyond everything."

Rachel proceeded to read the epistle; and for once Mona found herself in absolute accord with her cousin. Rachel's niece was certainly "no great hand at the letter-writing."

It was evening, and Mona had just come in from a stroll in the twilight. She did not often go out after tea, but there was no denying the fact that the last few days had not been very lively ones, and that physical exercise had become more desirable than ever. She had not realised, till he was gone, that Dr Dudley's occasional companionship made any appreciable difference in the world at Borrowness; but she did not now hesitate for a moment to acknowledge the truth to herself.

"It is almost as if I had lost Doris or Lucy," she said; "and of course, in a place like this, sympathetic companionship is at a premium. One might go into a melancholia here over the loss of an intelligent dog or a favourite canary. The fact that so many women have fallen in love throws a lurid light on the lives they must have led. Poor souls! I will write to Tilbury to-morrow to send me my little box of books. Two hours' hard reading a-day is a panacea for most things."

With this wholesome resolution she returned from her walk, to find Rachel in a state of beatification over her niece's letter.

"I declare I quite forgot," she said; "there's a parcel and letter for you too. I think you'll find them on the chair by the door."

" Nothing of much interest," said Mona ; " at least I don't know the handwriting on either. A begging-letter, I expect."

She proceeded to open the parcel first, untying the knot very deliberately, and speculating vaguely as to the cause of the curious damp smell about the wrappings. " Fancy Ruching" in gilt letters on one end of the box was apparently a misleading title ; for, when the cover was removed, a mass of damp vegetation came to view.

Rachel lifted her hands in horror. The idea of bringing caterpillars and earwigs and the like of that into the house !

On the top of the box lay a sheet of moist writing - paper folded lengthwise. Mona took it up.

" Why," she said, " how very kind ! It is from Mr Brown. He has been out botanising, and has sent me the fruits of an afternoon's ramble."

" The man must be daft !" thought Rachel, " to pay the postage on stuff that anybody else would put on the ash-heap. The very box isn't fit to use after having that rubbish inside it."

Fortunately, before she could give utterance to her thoughts, a brilliant idea flashed into her mind. Regarded absolutely, the box might be rubbish ; but relatively, it might prove to be of enormous value.

Everybody knew that the draper was " daft "; but nobody considered him any the less eligible in consequence, either as a provost or as a husband. For the matter of that, Mona was " daft " too. She cared as much about these bits of weed and stick as the draper did. There would be a pair of them in that respect. And then—how wonderfully things do come about in life !—Mona would find a field for her un- deniable gifts in the shopkeeping line. At Mr Brown's things were done on as large a scale as even she could desire ; and if she were called upon some day to fill the proud position of " Provost's lady," what other girl in the place would look the part so well ?

Of course the house at Borrowness would be sadly dull without her. But she might want to go away some time in any case, and at Kil- winnie she would always be within reach. Rachel would not admit even to herself that it might almost be a relief in some ways to be

delivered from the quiet thoughtful look of
those bright young eyes.

She beamed, and glowed, and would have
winked, if there had been any one but Mona
to wink to. With her of course she must
dissemble, till things had got on a little farther.
In the meantime, Mr Brown, quiet as he looked,
seemed quite capable of fighting his own battles;
though if any one had sent *her* such a box in
her young days, she would have regarded it in
the light of a mock valentine.

She longed to know what Mr Brown had
said ; but, when Mona handed her the letter,
she found it sadly disappointing. In so far
as it was not written in an unknown tongue,
it seemed to be all about the plants ; and who
in the world had ever taken the trouble to give
such grand names to things that grew in every
potato-bed that was not properly looked after ?
But of course tastes did differ, and no doubt
daft people understood each other.

Poor Rachel ! This disappointment was
nothing to the one in store for her. Mona
had opened the " begging - letter," and had
turned white to the lips.

" I must start by the early train to-morrow,"

she said, "and try to catch the Flying Scotsman. A little friend of mine in London is very ill."

It had proved to be a begging-letter indeed, but not of the kind she had supposed. It came from Lucy's father, Mr Reynolds.

"The doctor says that Lucy is in no actual danger," he wrote, "but she adds that her temperature *must not go* any higher. The child is fretting so for you that I am afraid this alone is enough to increase the fever. She was not very well when she left us to return to London a week ago; but our country doctor assured me there was no reason to keep her at home. Of course, Lucy had sent for a woman doctor before I arrived; and cordially as I approve her choice, a moment like this seems to call one's old prejudices, with other morbid growths, to life. Dr Alice Bateson seems very capable and is most attentive, but I need not deny that it would be a great relief to me to have you here. Lucy's mother is too much of an invalid to travel so far, and you have been like an elder sister to her for years.

"I know well that I need not apologise for the trouble to which I am putting you. I fully expect my little girl to improve from the moment she hears that I have written."

Mona read this aloud, adding, " I will go out and telegraph to him at once."

" Well, I'm sure," said Rachel, " it's a deal of trouble to take for a mere acquaintance—not even a blood relation."

" Lucy is more than a mere acquaintance," said Mona, with a quiver in her voice. " She has been, as he says, a little sister."

" What does he say is the matter ? "

" Rheumatic fever."

" Then," said Rachel, bitterly, " I suppose I may send your boxes after you ? "

" No, no," said Mona, forcing herself to speak playfully ; " a bargain is a bargain, and I mean to keep you to yours. Six months is in the bond. I will come back as soon as Lucy is well on the way to recovery—within a week, I hope. You know rheumatic fever is not the lengthy affair that it used to be. I assure you, dear, a visit to London is the very last thing I want at present. So far as I personally am concerned, I would infinitely rather stay with you. But I am not of so much use here that I should refuse to go to people who really need me."

If she wanted a crumb of encouragement, she was not disappointed, although Rachel was one of the people who do not find it easy to grant such crumbs.

"Well, I'm sure that's just what you are," she said. "I don't know what I am to do without you, and everybody says the shop has been a different place since you came." With a great effort she refrained from referring to stronger reasons still against Mona's departure.

Mona kissed her on the forehead.

"Then expect me back this day week or sooner," she said. "You don't want me more than I want to come."

This was the literal truth. When she had laid her plans, she was not grateful to the unfriendly Fates who interfered with their execution; she was honestly interested in her life at Borrowness; and it was a positive trial to return to London, a deserter at least for the time, just when all the scholastic world, with bustle and stir, was preparing for a new campaign.

She went to the post-office and sent off her telegram to Mr Reynolds, and another to Doris announcing the fact that she was going to

London for a few days, and would be at the Waverley Station before ten the next morning. This done, she returned to the house, wrote a friendly note to Mr Brown, packed her valise, and spent the rest of the evening with Rachel and " Mrs Poyser."

She did not pass a very peaceful night. It was all very well to say that Lucy's temperature "must not go any higher"; but what if it did? If it had continued to rise ever since the letter was written, what might be the result even now? Mona had seen several such cases in hospital, and she remembered one especially, in which cold baths, ice-packs, and all other remedies had not been sufficient to prevent a lad's life from being burnt out in a few days. She tossed restlessly from side to side, and what sleep she got was little better than a succession of nightmares. She was thankful to rise even earlier than was necessary, and to busy herself with some of Mr Brown's specimens.

But, early as she was, Rachel was up before her, cutting bulky, untempting sandwiches; and when the train carried Mona away, an unexpected tear coursed down the flabby old cheek.

On the platform at Edinburgh stood Doris, fresh as a lily.

"It's very good of you to come," said Mona. "I did not half expect to see you."

"My dear," was the calm announcement, "I am going all the way."

"Nonsense!"

"Father remarked most opportunely that I seemed to be in need of a little change, and I gave him no peace till he allowed me to come with you. He admitted that such an opportunity might not occur again. He would have been here to see us off, but he had a big consultation at ten. You will show me the school and the hospital and everything, won't you?"

"That I will," said Mona.

That she would at all have preferred to keep away from her old haunts and companions, just at present, never crossed the mind of large-souled Doris. "Mona capable of such pettiness!" she would have said in reply to the suggestion. "You little know her!"

"One has not much space for *minutiæ* in a telegram," said Mona, "or I would have explained that I am going to see a friend who is very ill. You have heard me speak of Lucy Reynolds?"

"Oh, I am sorry! But I shall not be in your way, you know. If you can spare a few hours some day, that is all I want."

"It is a matter of no moment of course, but do you happen to have any notion where you mean to put up?"

"I shall go to my aunt in Park Street of course, the one whose 'At Homes' you so loftily refused to attend. Father telegraphed to her last night, and I got a very cordial reply before I started. In point of fact, she is always glad to have me without notice. We don't stand on ceremony on either side."

"Well, you are a delightful person! I know no one who can do such sensible, satisfactory things without preliminary fuss. Shall we take our seats?"

"I took the seats long ago—two nice window seats in a third-class carriage. Your friend the 'pepper-pot' has duly deposited my wraps in one, and my dressing-bag in the other, and is now mounting guard in case of accident. You have plenty of time to have a cup of coffee at Spiers & Pond's."

In a few minutes they seated themselves in the carriage, dismissed the "pepper-pot," and launched into earnest conversation. Not till the train was starting did Mona raise her eyes, and then they alighted on a friendly, familiar figure. At the extreme end of the platform stood the Sahib. All unaware that she was in the train, he was waving his hat to some one else, his fine muscular figure reducing all the other men on the platform, by force of contrast, to mere pigmies.

When Mona saw him it was too late even to bow, and she turned away from the window, her face flushed with disappointment.

"Oh, Doris," she said, "that was the Sahib!"

"And who," asked Doris, "may the Sahib be?"

"A Mr Dickinson. I saw a good deal of him in Norway this summer. He is a great friend of the Munros, you know. Such a good fellow! The sort of man whom all women instinctively look upon as a brother."

"The type is a rare one," said Doris, coldly, "but I suppose it does exist."

The conversation had struck the vein of her cynicism now, though the men who knew "the lily maid" would have been much surprised to hear that such a vein existed, and, most of all, to hear that it lay just there.

"I don't think any of us can doubt that there is such a type," said Mona. "Certainly no one doubts it who has the privilege of knowing the Sahib."

Doris did not answer, and they sat for some time in silence, the line on Mona's brow gradually deepening.

"Dearest," said Doris at last, "I don't bore you, do I? You would not rather be alone?"

Mona laughed. "What will you do if I say 'Yes'?" she said. "Pull the cord and pay the fine? or jump out of the window? My dear, I could count on the fingers of one hand the times when you have bored me, and I am particularly glad to have you to-day. I should fret myself to death if I were alone, between anxiety about Lucy, and vexation at having missed the Sahib."

Doris's face clouded. "Mona dear, I do wish the Munros had stayed in India till you had got on the Register. I don't approve of men whom all women instinctively look upon as brothers. Marriage is perfectly fatal to students of either sex."

"Marriage!" said Mona, aghast. "Marry the Sahib! My dear Doris, I would as soon think of marrying you!"

"I wish you would," said Doris, calmly; "but I would not have a word to say to you till you had got on the Register. Oh how lovely!"

The train had emerged on the open coast, and every line and curve on creek and cliff stood out sharp and clear in the crisp light of the October morning.

"Isn't it?" The line on Mona's brow vanished. "You know, Doris, I believe I am a bit of the east coast, I love it so. Heigh-ho! I do think Lucy must be better."

"Judging from what you have told me of her, I should think the chances were in favour of her meeting you at the station."

Mona laughed. "She *is* an india-rubber ball —up one moment, down the next; but it has been no laughing matter this time. I told you *she* got through her examination all right."

"Thanks to your coaching, no doubt."

"No, no, no! I begin to think Lucy has a better head all round than mine. The fact is, Doris, I have to readjust my views of life some-

how, and the only satisfactory basis on which I
can build is the conviction that we have all been
under a complete misapprehension as to my
powers.   There is something gloriously restful
in the belief that one is nothing great, and is
not called upon to do anything particular."

Doris smiled with serene liberality.   Mona
had been in her mind constantly during the
last month.

"Very well," she said.   "As long as you feel
like that, go your own way.   I am not afraid
that the mood will last.   In a few months you
will be neither to hold nor to bind."

"Prophet of evil!"

"Nay; prophet of good."

"It is all very well for you, in your lovely
leisure, realising the ideal of perfect womanhood."

"Don't be sarcastic, please.   You know how
gladly I would exchange my 'lovely leisure'
for your freedom to work.   But we need not
talk of it.   My mind is perfectly at rest about
you.   This is only a reaction—a passing phase."

"A great improvement on the restless, hound-
ing desire to inflict one's powers, talents, and
virtues—save the mark!—on poor, patient, long-

suffering mankind. Oh, Doris, let us take life simply, and work our reformations unconsciously by the way. We don't increase our moral energy by pumping our resolutions up to a giddy height."

" I am not to remind you, I suppose, of the old gospel which some of your friends associate with you, that women ought always to have a purpose in life, and not be content to drift."

Mona turned a pair of laughing eyes full on her friend.

" Remind me of it by all means. Go a stage farther back, if you like, and remind me of my dolls. I am not sensitive on either point. I was saying to some one only the other day that it takes a great many incompatible utterances to make up a man's *Credo*, even at one moment. Perhaps," she added more slowly, " each of us is, in potentiality, as catholic as God Himself on a small scale ; but owing to the restrictions and mutual pressure of human life, most of us can only develop one side at a time—some of us only one in a single ' Karma.' "

" You seem," said Doris, quietly, " to have found the intellectual life at Borrowness at a surprisingly high level."

Mona raised her eyebrows with a quick, unconscious gesture.

"There are a few intelligent people," she said, rather coldly, "even there."

"But, Mona, your life has been so free from restriction and pressure. You have been able to develop on the lines you chose."

"Don't argue that my responsibility is the greater! How do we know that it is not the less? Besides, there may be very real pressure and restriction, which is invisible even to the most sympathetic eye."

"I don't want to argue at all. I don't profess to follow all your flights; but I am perfectly satisfied that you will come back to the point you started from."

Mona rose and took down a plaid from the rack. "Make it a spiral, Doris, if you conscientiously can," she said, gravely. "I don't like moving in a circle. 'Build thee more stately mansions, O my soul!'"

Doris looked admiringly at her friend. She could very conscientiously have "made it a spiral," but she was not in the habit of talking in metaphors as Mona was.

The conversation dropped, and they sat for

a long time listening to the rattle and roar of
the train. Mona did not like it. Somehow it
forced her to remember that there was no necessary connection between Lucy's condition and
the bright October weather.

"A penny for your thoughts, Doris," she
cried.

Doris's large grey eyes were sparkling.

"I was wondering," she said, "whether that
delicious seal is still at the Zoo. Do you
know?"

"I don't; you might as well ask me whether
Carolus Rex is still brandishing his own death-
warrant at Madame Tussaud's."

"Picture mentioning the two places on the
same day!"

"I do it because they lie side by side in the
fairy memory palace of childhood. Neither has
any existence for me apart from that."

"And you a student of natural history! I
should have thought that most of your spare
time would have been spent at the Zoological
Gardens."

"*Ars longa!*—but you are perfectly right.
The Huxley of the next generation, instead of
directing us to scalpel and dissecting-board, will

tell us to forego the use of those, till we have
studied the build and movements and habits of
the animals in life. I quite agree with you
that it is far better to know and love the
creatures as you do, than to investigate personally the principal variations of the ground-
plan of the vascular system, as I do."

" I don't see why we should not combine
the two."

" Truly; but something else would have to
go to the wall; Turner, perhaps, or Browning,
or Wagner.

'We have not wings, we cannot soar;
But we have feet to scale and climb.'"

" I don't know. Some of us appear to have
discovered a pretty fair substitute for wings.
But you know I am looking forward to your
dissecting-room far more even than to the Zoological Gardens."

" You don't really mean to see the dissecting-
room ?"

" Of course I do. Why not ?"

" Chiefly, I suppose, because you never can
see it. No outsider can form any conception
of what the dissecting-room really is. You

would only be horrified at the ghastliness of it,
—shocked that young girls can laugh over such
work."

"Do they laugh?" said Doris, in an awestruck
tone. She had pictured to herself heroic self-
abnegation; but laughter!

"Of course they do, if there is anything to
laugh at. We laughed a great deal at an Irish
girl who could only remember the nerves of the
arm by ligaturing them with different-coloured
threads. When girls are doing crewel-work, or
painting milking-stools, they are not incessantly
thinking of the source of their materials. No
more are we."

"But it is so different."

"Is it? I don't know. If it is, a merciful
Providence shuts our eyes to the difference. It
simply becomes *our work*, sacred or commonplace, according to our character and way of
looking at things. There are minor disagreeables, of course; but what pursuit is without
them? And if they are greater in practical
anatomy than in other things, there is increased
interest to make up for them."

"Oh yes, I am sure of that. I think nothing
of disagreeables in such a cause. And I suppose

what you say is very natural; but I always
fancied that lofty enthusiasm would be necessary to carry one through."

"I think lofty enthusiasm is necessary to carry
us nobly through anything. But lofty enthusiasm
is not an appendage to wear at one's finger-ends;
it is the heart, the central pump of the whole
system, about which we never think till we
grow physically or morally morbid. You know,
dear, I don't mean to say that the dissecting-
room is pleasant from the beginning. Before
one really gets into the work it is worse than
ghastly, it is *awful*. That is why I say that
outsiders should never see it. For the first few
days, I used to clench my teeth, and repeat to
myself over and over again, 'After life's fitful
fever, he sleeps well.' It sounds ironical, does
not it? But it comforted me. On any theory
of life, *this* struggle was over for one poor soul;
and, judging by the net result in this world, it
must have been a sore and bitter struggle. But
you know I could not have gone on like that;
it would have killed me. I had to cease thinking about it at all in that way, and look upon
it simply as my daily work—sometimes commonplace, sometimes enthralling. Sir Douglas

would say I grew hardened, but I don't think I did."

" Hardened !" said Doris, her own eyes softening in sympathy as she watched Mona's lips quiver at the bare recollection of those days. " How like a man ! "

" I never spoke of this before, except once when my uncle made me ; but if you are determined to go in——"

" Oh yes, I mean to see all I can. You don't object very much, do you ? "

" Object ? " Mona's earnestness had all gone. " Did you ever know me object to anything ? I did not even presume to advise ; I only stated an opinion in the abstract. But here is York, and luncheon. We can continue the conversation afterwards."

But the conversation was over for that day. Just as the train was about to start, Doris leaned out of the window.

" Oh, Mona," she said, " here is a poor woman with four little children, looking for a carriage that will hold them all. Poor soul ! She does look hot and tired. I do wish she would look in our direction. Here she comes ! "

Doris threw open the door, and lifted the children and bundles in, one by one.

" You did not mind, did you ? " she said suddenly to Mona, as the train moved on.

" Oh no ! " Mona laughed, and shrugged her shoulders. " One must pay the penalty of travelling with a *schöne Seele !* "

CHAPTER XXII.

DR ALICE BATESON.

GLARING lights in the murky darkness, hurrying porters pursuing the train, eager eyes on the platform strained in the direction of the windows, announced the arrival of the Flying Scotsman at King's Cross.

"Are you sure your husband will be here to meet you?" said Doris to her *protégée*. "I will stay with the children till you find him. Mona, dear, I had better say good night. I will call to-morrow morning to see you and inquire for your friend."

"Is there any one here to meet you?"

"I saw my aunt's footman a minute ago. He will find me presently."

A moment later a beautiful, white-haired old clergyman came up, removing his glove before shaking hands with Mona.

" I scarcely know how to thank you," he said, in a low voice.   " You are a friend in need."

" And Lucy ? "

" Lucy's temperature, as I expected, has gone down with a run since she heard you were coming.   The doctor says all will be well now."

Mona drew a long breath of relief, and looked up in his face with a smile.

He laid his hand on her shoulder.   " Where is your luggage ? "

" This porter has my valise.   That is all."

They got into a hansom, while the tall foot-man conducted Doris to a neat brougham, and a moment later they rattled away.

If Sir Douglas made Mona " a girl again," Mr Reynolds made her feel herself a child.   With him her superficial crust of cynicism vanished like hoar-frost before the sun, and gave place to a gentle deference which had completely won the old man's heart.   " The type of woman I admire," he had said with dignity to Lucy, " is the woman of clear intellect ; " but it is probable that the woman of clear intellect would have appealed to him less, if she had not looked at him with pathetic revering eyes that seemed to say, "They call me clever and strong, but I am only a fatherless girl after all."

"Will Lucy be settled for the night when we get home?" Mona asked, when she had exhausted her other questions.

"No; she gets a hypodermic injection of morphia when the pain comes on, and that was to be postponed, if possible, till our arrival."

In a few minutes the cab drew up at a dimly lighted door in Bloomsbury. The house was old-fashioned and substantial; but a certain air of squalor is inseparably associated with most London lodgings, and it was not altogether absent here.

"Will you show this lady to her room?" said the clergyman courteously to the maid who opened the door.

"Not yet, thank you," said Mona. "Show me to Miss Reynolds's room, please. I will go there first."

The room was brightly lighted with a pretty lamp, for Lucy could not bear to have anything gloomy about her. She was lying in bed, propped up with pillows, her eyes curiously large and bright, her cheeks thin, her face worn with recent suffering.

Mona bit her lip hard. She had not realised that a few days of fever and pain could work such a change.

Lucy tried to stretch out her arms, and then let them fall with a pitiful little laugh. "I can't hug you yet, Mona," she said, "but oh! it is good to see you," and tears of sheer physical weakness filled her eyes.

"You poor little thing! What a scolding you shall have when you are better! You are not to be trusted out of my sight for a moment."

"I know," said Lucy, feebly. "I never should have got ill if you had been here; and now I shall just have one illness after another, till you come back and go on with your work."

She looked so infinitely pathetic and unlike herself that Mona could scarcely find words. Instinctively she took Lucy's wrist in one cool hand, and laid the other on the child's flushed cheek.

"Oh, I am all right now. Of course my heart bounded off when I heard the hansom stop. But here comes my doctor. I scarcely need you to send me to Paradise to-night, doctor; my friend Miss Maclean has come."

Mona held out her hand. " Your name is almost as familiar to me as my own," she said. " It is a great pleasure to meet you."

Dr Alice Bateson took the proffered hand without replying, and the two women exchanged a frank critical survey. Both seemed to be satisfied with the result. Dr Bateson had come in without gloves, and with a shawl thrown carelessly about her girlish figure. Her hat had seen palmier days, but its bent brim shaded a pair of earnest brown eyes and a resolute mouth.

" She means work," thought Mona. " There is no humbug about her."

" The girl has some *nous*," thought the doctor. " She would keep her head in an emergency."

" Well, and how are you ? " she said, turning with brusque kindness to Lucy.

" Oh, I am all right—not beyond the need of your stiletto yet, though," and she held out a pretty white arm.

The medical visit did not last more than three minutes. Dr Bateson took no fees from medical students, and she had too many patients on her books to waste much time over them, unless there seemed to be a chance that she could be of definite use, physical or moral. She had spent hours with Lucy when things were at their worst, but minutes were ample now.

"Oh yes. Miss Reynolds will do famously," she said to Mona, who had left the room with her. "Fortunately I was close at hand, and she sent for me in time. With a temperament like hers, the temperature runs up and down very readily, and it went up so quickly that I was rather uneasy, but it never reached a really alarming height. Good night, Miss Maclean. I hope we shall see you at 'The New' before long."

"Thank you; there is nothing I should like better than to work under you at the Women's Hospital," and Mona ran back to Lucy's room.

"Now, my baby," she said, caressingly, "I will arrange your pillows, and you shall go to sleep like a good child."

"Sleep," said Lucy, dreamily. "I don't *sleep*. I go through the looking-glass into the queerest, most fantastic world you can imagine. *C'est magnifique—mais—ce n'est pas—le—sommeil.*" She roused herself with a slight effort. "About three I go to sleep, and don't wake till ten. How good it will be to see you beside me in the morning!"

Mr Reynolds came into the room, kissed the little white hand that lay on the counterpane, and then gave Mona his arm.

"You poor child," he said, as they left the room together, "you must be worn out and faint. That is your room, and the sitting-room is just at the foot of the stair. I will leave the door open. Supper is waiting."

A very pleasant hour the two spent together. Mona was at her best with Mr Reynolds,— simple, earnest, off her guard; and as for the clergyman, he was almost always at his best now.

"I felt quite sure you would come," he said, "but I am ashamed to think of the trouble to which you have been put. I hope you have not had a very tiresome journey?"

"I have had a most pleasant journey from Edinburgh. My friend Doris Colquhoun came with me."

"Was that the fair young lady with the children? I was going to ask if you knew her. She had a very pleasing face."

"Yes; the children don't belong to her, but she has been mothering their weary mother. Doris is such a good woman. She does not care a straw for the petty personal things that most of us are occupied with. Even home comforts are a matter of indifference to her. But for animals, and poor women, and the cause of the oppressed generally, she has the enthusiasm of a martyr."

" She looks a mere girl."

" She is about my age; but she is so much less self-centred than I am, that she has always seemed to me a good deal older. She is my mother-confessor, and far too indulgent for the post."

" ' A heart at leisure from itself ' ? "

" Yes, that is Doris all over. I don't believe she ever passed a sleepless night for sorrows of her own. By the way, Lucy says the morphia does not make her sleep."

" So she says, but it seems difficult to draw the line between sleeping and waking when one is under opium. I shall be thankful when Lucy can dispense with the drug, though I shall never forget my gratitude when I first saw the doctor administer it. It seemed to wipe out the pain as a wet sponge wipes out the marks on a slate."

" I know. There is nothing like it. We had

a case in hospital of a man who was stabbed in the body. Modern surgery might have saved him, but he came into hospital too late, and they kept him more or less under morphia till the end. Whenever he began to come out of it, he wailed, 'Give me morphia, give me morphia!' and, oh, how unspeakably thankful one was that there was morphia to give him!"

The old man sighed. "It is a difficult subject, the 'mystery of pain.' We believe in its divine mission, and yet our theories vanish in the actual presence of it. When pain has been brought on by sin and folly, and seems morally to have a distinct remedial value, we should surely be very slow to relieve it ; and yet how can we, seeing as we do only one little span of existence, judge of remedial value, except on a very small scale ? "

"And therefore," said Mona, deprecatingly, " we should surely err on the safe side, and be merciful, except in a case that is absolutely clear even to our finite eyes. At the best, the wear and tear of pain lowers our stamina— makes us less fit for the battle of life, more open to temptation."

He sighed again.

"'So runs my dream, but what am I?
    An infant crying in the night!'

Ah, well! if we can say at the last day, 'I was
not wise, but I tried to be merciful,' I think
we shall find forgiveness; and, if we are to
find peace and acceptance, so surely must all
those whom we have wittingly or unwittingly
wronged."

Pleasant as the evening was, Mr Reynolds
insisted on making it a very short one.

"No, no. Indeed you shall not sit up with
Lucy to-night. You want rest as much as she
does. If she still needs any one to-morrow, we
will talk about it, but she is progressing by
strides." He kissed Mona on the forehead, and
she went to her own room, to sleep a long
dreamless sleep, broken only by the entrance
of the hot water next morning.

CHAPTER XXIII.

A RENCONTRE.

TRUE to her promise, Doris called before eleven.

"Well, this is a surprise," said Mona. "I did not in the least expect to see you."

"Why? I said I would come."

"Yes; but I thought you would go off to visit that woman, and forget all about me. What is old friendship when weighed against the misfortune of being 'hadden doon' of a husband and four children!"

"The man was a selfish brute," said Doris, ignoring an imputation she would have resented if her mind had been less full of other things. "Did you notice? He let his wife carry more than half the bundles. I sent John to take them from her, and fortunately that put him to shame."

"And how did John like it?"

Doris laughed. "Oh, I don't know; I never thought of him. I think John is rather attached to me."

"I have yet to meet the man in any rank of life who knows you and is not attached to you. I think that has taught me more of the nature of men than any other one thing. They little dream of the contempt and scorn that lie behind that daisy face, and yet they seem to know by a sort of instinct that their charms are thrown away on you,—that the fruit is out of reach; and instead of sensibly saying 'sour grapes,' they knock themselves to pieces against the wall."

"Mona, you do talk nonsense! I have scarcely had an offer of marriage in my life."

"I imagine that few women who really respect themselves have more than one, unless the men of their acquaintance—like the population of the British Isles—are 'mostly fools.'"

"Oh, they are all that. But I think what you say is very true. The first offer comes like a slap in the face, 'out of the everywhere.' Who could have foreseen it? But after that one gets to know when there is electricity in the air, don't you think so?"

" I suppose so. But the experience is not much in my line. Sensible men are rather apt to think me a *guter Kamerad*, and one weakminded young curate asked me to share two hundred a-year with him—his 'revenue' he called it, by the way. Behold the extent of my dominion over the other sex! I sometimes think," she added, gloomily, " it is commensurate with the extent to which I have attained the ideal of womanhood!"

" Mona! If the sons of God were to take unto themselves wives of the daughters of men, we should hear a different tale. As things are, I am glad you are not a man's woman. You are a woman's woman, which is infinitely better. If you could be turned into a man to-morrow, half the girls of your acquaintance would marry you. I know I would, for one."

" You are my oldest friend, Doris," said Mona, gratefully. " The others like me because I am moody and mysterious, and occasionally motherly. Women always fall in love with the Unknown."

" How could they marry men if it were otherwise?" said Doris, but she did not in the least mean it for wit.

"You miserable old cynic! I am going to introduce you to-day—I say advisedly introduce *you*—to a man who will convert even Doris Colquhoun to a love of his sex. He met me at the station last night, but I suppose you were too much taken up with your *protégées* to notice him."

"I caught a glimpse of white hair and an old-world bow. One can't judge of faces in the glaring light and black shadows of a railway station at night."

"That's true. Everybody looks like an amateur photograph taken indoors. But you shall see Mr Reynolds to-day. He promised to come in. Present company excepted, I don't know that I love any one in the world as I do him—unless it be Sir Douglas Munro."

"Sir Douglas Munro! Oh Mona! I heard my father say once that Sir Douglas was a good fellow, but that no one could look at him and doubt that he had sown his wild oats very thoroughly."

"*Don't!*" said Mona, with a little stamp of her foot. "Why need we think of it? I cannot even tell you how kind he has been to me."

Doris was about to reply, but Mr Reynolds

came in at the moment, and they chatted on general topics for a few minutes. "Dr Alice Bateson has just come in," he said, in answer to Doris's inquiry after Lucy.

Doris's face flushed. "Oh," she said, eagerly, "I should so like to meet Dr Alice Bateson."

"Should you?" he said, with a fatherly smile. "That is easily managed. We will open the door and waylay her as she comes down. Ah, doctor! here is a young lady from Scotland who is all anxiety to make your acquaintance. May I introduce her?"

Miss Bateson came in. She did not at all like to be made a lion of, but Doris's fair, eager face was irresistible.

"I am very glad," Doris said, shyly, "to express my personal thanks to any woman who is helping on what I consider one of the noblest causes in the world."

"It is a grand work," said Dr Bateson, rather shortly. "Miss——" she looked at Mona.

"Maclean," said Mona, with a smile.

"Miss Maclean will be able to show you our School and Hospital. Perhaps we may meet some day at the Hospital. Good morning."

"Well?" said Mona, when she was gone.

"I think she is splendid—so energetic and sensible. But, you know, I do wish she wore gloves; and she would look so nice in a bonnet."

"Come, don't be narrow-minded."

"I am not narrow-minded. Personally I like her all the better for her unconventionality. It is the Cause I am thinking of."

"Oh, the Cause! It seems to me, dear, that the prophets of great causes always have a thorn in the flesh that they themselves are conscious of, and half-a-dozen other thorns that other people are conscious of; but the cause survives notwithstanding."

"I have no doubt that it will survive; but it seems to me that a little care on the part of the prophets would make it grow so much faster. Well, dear, I must go. I will come again on Friday. You will come to my aunt's 'At Home,' won't you?"

"If Lucy is better, and your aunt gives me another chance, I shall be only too glad. I shall have to unearth a gown from my boxes at Tilbury's. Heigh-ho, Doris! I might as well have gone all along, for all the good my abstinence did me. A deal of wasted pluck and moral courage goes to failing in one's Intermediate M.B. !"

"You have been gone a quarter of an hour," said Lucy, fretfully, when Mona re-entered the sick-room, "and Miss Colquhoun had you all day yesterday."

"You are getting better, little woman," said Mona, kissing her.

"We have so much to talk about——"

"So we have, dear, but not to-day, nor yet to-morrow. I won't have my coming throw you back. You are to eat all the milk and eggs and nursery pudding that you possibly can, and I will read you the last new thing in three-volume novels."

Lucy resigned herself to this *régime* the more readily as she was too weak to talk; and she certainly did make remarkable progress in the next day or two. She was very soon able— rather to her own disappointment—to do without morphine at night; and when, a few days later, Mona read the last page of the novel, Lucy was lying in a healthy natural sleep.

Mona stole out of the room, listened outside the door for a minute or two, and then ran down-stairs.

"I hope you are going out?" said Mr Reynolds, looking up from his *Guardian*. "You have been shut up for three or four days now."

"Yes; I told Lucy that if she went to sleep I would go for a run. She is to ring as soon as she wakes."

"Well, don't hurry back. I expect the child will sleep all the afternoon; and if she does not, she may content herself with the old man's company for an hour or two."

"Lucky girl!" said Mona, looking at him affectionately. "I should think 'the old man's company' would more than make up to most people for being ill."

Lucy's fellow-students had called regularly to inquire for her, and this Friday morning a bright young girl had come in on her way to the Medical School, at the same moment as Doris Colquhoun.

"I only wish I were going with you," Doris had said to her; and Mona had thankfully availed herself of the opportunity so to arrange matters.

"I will go and have tea with Doris now," she thought, "and hear all her impressions before their edge has worn off."

She set off in high spirits. After all, it was very pleasant to be in London again, especially in this bright cold weather. The shop-windows still had all their old attraction, and she stopped every few minutes to look at the new winter fads and fashions, wondering what pretty things it would be well to take back to Borrowness; for Rachel had reluctantly consented to the investment of a few pounds in fresh stock-in-trade.

"Whatever I buy will be hideously out of keeping with everything else," thought Mona; "but a shop ought to be a shop before it professes to be a work of art. At present it is what Dr Dudley would call 'nayther fish, flesh, fowl, nor guid red herrin'.'"

She had taken the measure of her *clientèle* at Borrowness pretty correctly, and she had a very good idea what things would appeal to their fancy, without offending her own somewhat fastidious taste; but she took as much pride in making the most of those pounds as if her own bread and cheese had depended on it. "We will do nothing hastily, my dear," she said to herself. "We will exhaust all the possibilities before we commit ourselves to the extent of one shilling. Oh dear, I am glad I

have not to go to the School after all! I am in
no mood for fencing."

Rash thought! It had scarcely passed through
her mind before a voice behind her said—

"How do you do, Miss Maclean?" and looking round she saw two of her fellow-students,
bag in hand.

As ill-luck would have it, one of them was
the only student of her own year with whom
Mona had always found herself absolutely out
of sympathy. This one it was who spoke.

"It is a surprise to see you! Miss Reynolds
said you were not coming back this winter."

"Nor am I. I am only in town for a day
or two."

"Are you reading at home?"

"At present I am not reading at all."

"It seems a great pity."

"Do you think so? I think it does us no
harm to climb up occasionally on the ridge that
separates our little furrow from all the others,
and see what is going on in the rest of the
field."

"But you always did that, did you not? I
thought you were a great authority on the uses
of frivolling."

"And you thought it a pity that the results of my examinations did not do more to bear out my teaching? Never mind. It is only one of the many cases in which a worthy cause has suffered temporarily in the hands of an unworthy exponent."

The girl coloured. Mona's hypersensitive perception had read her thought very correctly.

"We miss you dreadfully," put in the other student, hastily. "I do wish you would come back."

"I suppose," continued the first, glancing at the shop-window before which they had met, "you are busy with your winter shopping. Regent Street has not lost its old attractions, though the Medical School has."

"What would they say," thought Mona, "if I calmly told them the whole truth?—that I am, with the utmost care and economy, buying goods for a very small shop in Borrowness, behind the counter of which I have the honour of standing, and serving a limited, and not very enlightened, public."

For a moment the temptation to "make their hair stand on end" was almost irresistible; but fortunately old habits of reserve are not broken

through in a moment, and she merely said, "Oh
no.   It will be a serious symptom when Regent
Street loses its attractions.   That would indeed
be a strong indication for quinine and cod-liver
oil, or any other treatment you can suggest
for melancholia.   Good-bye, and success to you
both!"

She shook hands—rather cavalierly with the
first, cordially with the second.   "*You* all
right?" she asked quietly, as they parted.

"Yes, thank you."

"She *is* queer," said the student who had
spoken first, when Mona was out of hearing.
"My private opinion is that she is going to be
married.   My brother saw her on board one of
the Fjord steamers in Norway a month or two
ago, with a very correct party; and he said a
tall fellow 'with tremendous calves' was paying
her a lot of attention."

"Did your brother speak to her?"

"No.   He was much smitten with her at the
last prize-giving, and wanted me to introduce
him, but I did not get a chance.   She knows
a lot of people.   I think she gives herself
tremendous airs, don't you?"

"I used to, but I began to think last term

that that was a mistake. You know, Miss Burnet, I like her."

"I don't."

"The fact is,"—the girl coloured and drew a long breath,—"I know you won't repeat it, but I have much need to like her. I was in frightful straits for money last term. I actually had a summons served upon me. I could not tell my people at home, and one night, when I was simply in despair, I went to Miss Maclean. I did not like her, but borrowers can afford even less than beggars to be choosers, and she always seemed to have plenty of money. She was by no means the first person I had applied to, and I had ceased to expect anything but refusals. Well, I shall never forget how her face lighted up as she said, 'How good of you to come to me! I know what it is to be short of money myself.' I did not think she gave herself airs then; I would have worked my fingers to the bone, if it had been necessary, to pay her back before the end of term."

"I don't see anything so wonderful in that. She had the money, and you had not."

"That's all very well. Wait till you have been refused by half-a-dozen people who could quite afford to help you. Wait till you have been treated to delightful theories on the evils of borrowing, when you are half frantic for the want of a few pounds."

"I am sure Miss Maclean wastes money enough. I was in the pit at the Lyceum one night, and I saw her and Miss Reynolds in the stalls. I am quite sure none of the money came out of Miss Reynolds' pocket."

"Miss Reynolds is a highly favoured person. I quite admit that there is nothing wonderful about *her*. But I like Miss Maclean, and if she gives up Medicine she will be a terrible loss."

"She has been twice ploughed."

"The more shame to the examiners!"

"Doris," said Mona a few minutes later, as she entered the æsthetic drawing-room where her friend was sitting alone at tea, "stay me with Mazawattee and comfort me with crumpets, for I have just met my *bête noire.*"

Doris looked up with a bright smile of welcome. "Come," she said, "'don't be narrow-minded'!"

Mona took up a down cushion and threw it at her friend.

"Pick that up, please," said Doris, quietly. "If my aunt comes in and sees her new Liberty cushion on the floor, it will be the end of you, so far as her good graces are concerned."

Mona picked it up, half absently, and replaced it on the sofa.

"Well, go on. Tell me all about your *bête noire*. Who is he?"

"*He*, of course! How is one to break it to you, dear Doris, that every member of our charming sex is not at once a Hebe and a Minerva?"

"I will try to bear up—remembering that 'God Almighty made them to match the men.' Proceed."

But Mona did not proceed at once. She drank her tea and looked fierce.

"I *am* narrow-minded," she said at last. "I wish that any power, human or divine, would prevent all women from studying medicine till they are twenty-three, and any woman from studying it at all, unless she has some one qualification, physical, mental, moral, or social, for the work. These remarks do not come very aptly from one who has been twice ploughed, but we are among friends."

"Well, dear," said Doris, thoughtfully, "there

were a few students at the School to-day whom one could have wished to see—elsewhere; but on the whole, they struck me as a party of happy, healthy, sensible, hard-working girls."

"Did they?" said Mona, eagerly; "I am very glad."

"Yes, assuredly they did, and a few of them seemed to be really remarkable women."

"Oh yes! the exceptions are all right; but tell me about your visit. I wish you could have gone in summer, when they are sitting about in the garden with books and bones, and materia medica specimens."

"Two of them were playing tennis when I went in—playing uncommonly well too. We watched them for a while, and then we went to the dissecting-room."

"Well?"

"I am very glad you told me what you did about it—*very*. I think if I had gone quite un-prepared I might have found it very ghastly and very awful. It is painful, of course, but it is intensely interesting. The demonstrator is such a nice girl. She took me round and showed me the best dissections; I had no idea the things looked like that. Do you know "—Doris waxed triumphant—" I know what fascia is, and I know a tendon from a nerve, and both from a vein."

" You have done well. Some of us who have worked for years cannot say as much—in a difficult case."

" Don't mock me ; you know what I mean. Oh, Mona, how you can be in London and not go back to your work is more than I can imagine."

" Yes ? That is interesting, but not strictly to the point. What did you do when you left the dissecting-room ? "

" Attended a physiology lecture, delivered by a young man who kept his eyes on the ceiling, and never moved a muscle of his face, unless it was absolutely necessary."

" I know," said Mona, laughing ; " but he knew exactly what was going on in the room all the time, and was doubtless wondering who the new and intelligent student was. He is delightful."

" He seemed nice," said Doris, judicially, " and he certainly was very clever ; but it would be much better to have women lecturers."

" That's true. But not unless they did the work every whit as well as men. You must not forget, dear, that a good laundress helps on the 'cause' of women better than a bad doctor or lecturer."

"Oh, I know that. But there must be plenty of women capable of lecturing on physiology."

Mona shrugged her shoulders.

"More things go to making a good physiology lecturer than you imagine,—a great many more," she added, impressively.

Doris's face flushed.

"Not vivisection!" she exclaimed.

"Yes, vivisection. It may be that our modern science has gone off on an entirely wrong tack; it may be, as a young doctor said to me at Borrowness the other day, that we cannot logically stop short now of vivisecting human beings; but, as things are at present, I do not see how any man can conscientiously take an important lectureship on physiology, unless he does original work. I don't mean to say that he must be at that part of it all the time. Far from it. He may make chemical physiology or histology his specialty. But you see physiology is such a floating, growing, mobile science. It exists in no text-book. Photograph it one day, and the picture is unrecognisable the next. What the physiologist has to do is to plunge his mind like a thermometer into the world of physiological investigation, and register one thing one moment, and another thing the next. He need never carry on experiments on living animals before his students, but he must live in the midst of the growing science—or be a humbug. I thought once that I should like nothing better than to be a lecturer on physiology, but I see now that it is impossible," she shivered,— "although, you know, dear, vivisection, as it exists in the popular mind, is a figment of the imaginations of the anti-vivisectionists."

Doris did not reply. She could not bear to think that Mona did not judge wisely and truly; she tried to agree with her in most things; but this was a hard saying.

"What does the young doctor at Borrowness say to a woman doctor?" she asked, suddenly.

Mona winced. "He does not know that I am a medical student. Why should he?"

"Oh, Mona, you don't mean to say you have not told him! What an opportunity lost!"

"It is not my custom to go about ticketed,

dear; but, if you wish, you shall tie a label
round my neck."

"However, you will see him again. There is
no hurry."

"It is to be hoped not," said Mona, a little
bitterly; "and now, dear, I must go."

CHAPTER XXIV.

A CLINICAL REPORT.

LUCY was up—actually standing by the fire in her own room—and Lucy was as saucy as ever.

"I believe you have grown," said Mona, regarding her critically.

"I should think I had! I must be two inches taller at least. What do you think, Mona? I have had two offers of marriage this summer."

"That is not surprising. I never had much opinion of the intelligence of the other sex. I hope you refused them."

"I did; but I will accept the next man who asks me, even if he is a chimney-sweep, just to spite you."

"Poor chimney-sweep! But look here, Pussy, you should not stand so long. Sit down in the arm-chair, and let me wrap you up in the eiderdown. And put your feet on the stool—so! Comfy?"

"Very comfy, thanks."

"When you are strong enough, I want you to give me a full, particular, and scientific account of your illness. How came *you* by acute rheumatism? You are not a beef and beer man."

"Well, when I went home I was in the most tearing spirits for the first week, and then I gradually began to feel fit for nothing. No appetite, short breath, and all the rest of it. I knew all I wanted was a tonic, and I determined to prescribe one for myself, on the strength of an intimate acquaintance with Mitchell Bruce. As a preparatory step, in the watches of the night, I tried to run over the ingredients and doses of the preparations of iron; but for the life of me I could not remember them. Think of it! A month after the examination! I could not even remember that *pièce de résistance* — you know! — the 'cinchona bark, calumba root, cloves' thing."

"Compound tincture of cardamoms and tincture of orange - peel," completed Mona, mechanically.

"Of course. That's it. 'Macerated in pep-permint-water,' wasn't it? or something of that sort. However, it does not matter now that I have passed."

"Not in the least!"

"Well, while I meditated, mother sent for the doctor, a mere boy—ugh! If I had been seriously ill, I should have said, 'Welcome death!' and declined to see him; but it was only a question of a tonic, so I resigned myself. He prescribed hypophosphites, and said I was to have a slice off the roast, or a chop or something, and a glass of porter twice a-day."

"*Ah!*" said Mona.

"It was no use telling mother that the infant knew less than I did   He was 'the doctor,' and that was enough. His word was law. I will say this for him, that I did get stronger; but just before I came back to town, I began to feel ill in quite a different way; indescribably queer, and fidgety and wretched. Mother made me stick to the beef and porter, as if my soul's weal had depended on it, and we all hoped the change to London might do me good. Just at first, I did feel a little better, and one afternoon Marion Proctor asked me to go down the river with her, and I went. My white dress was newly washed, and I had just done up my hat for the sixth time this summer. You may say what you like, Mona, but I did look awfully nice."

" I don't doubt it."

" I did not take my waterproof, because it completely spoilt the general effect, and I was sure it would not rain; but, as I told you, a tremendous thunderstorm came on, and we were drenched."

" Oh, Lucy!"

" When we got back here, there was not a fire in the house, and, do what I would, I got thoroughly chilled. I was shivering so, and I felt so feverish, that Marion insisted on spending the night with me. She slept in the room you have, and I was to knock on the wall if I wanted her."

Lucy stopped and shivered.

" There, dear," said Mona, " you will tell me the rest another time. You are tiring yourself."

" No, I am not; I like to tell you. Mona, I woke at two in the morning with these words in my mind, 'The sufferings of the damned.' Don't call me irreverent. You don't know what it is. It took me *three-quarters of an hour* to get out of bed to knock for Marion, and the tears were running down my face like rain."

"My poor baby!" Mona got up and knelt down beside her; but Lucy was already laughing at the next recollection.

"Oh, Mona, I did not see the comedy of it then, but I shall never forget that sight. The glimmering candle—Marion shivering in her night-dress, her sleepy eyes blinking as she read from a medical book, 'Rheumatism is probably due to excess of sarcolactic acid in the blood'! as if I was not far past caring what it was due to! Good old Marion! she dressed herself at once, and at six she went for Dr Bateson. Of course with the dawn the pain just came within the limits of endurance; but when the doctor gave me morphia, I could have fallen down and worshipped her."

"You poor little girl! How I wish I had been here! Let me go, dear, a minute. It is time for your medicine."

"Nasty bitter-sweet stuff—I wish I could stop *that!*"

"Why? I am sure it has worked wonders. How I wish we knew exactly how it acts!"

Lucy laughed. "You are as bad as Marion," she said. "If you were on the rack, you would not trouble yourself to understand the mechanism that stopped the wheels, so long as they were stopped. I leave it to you, dear, to cultivate the infant bacillus on a nice little nutrient jelly, and then polish him off with a dilute solution of salicin."

"What we want now," said Mona, meditatively, stroking the curly red hair, "is to get back our baby face. How do we mean to set about it?"

Lucy made a little *moue*. "Dr Bateson said something about the south of France—such a waste of time! And Father says when I come back to London I am to live at the College Hall again."

"I am very glad to hear it. I always thought your leaving was a great mistake."

"Why, you lived in rooms yourself!"

"Oh, *I!* I am an old granny full of fads, and quite able to take care of myself."

"Your best friend could not deny that you are full of fads; and that reminds me, Mona, it is your innings now. I am 'dagging' to hear all about Borrowness, and the shop and your

cousin. Your last letter fell very flat on ex-
pectant spirits."

Mona went leisurely back to her chair.
"You see, dear," she said, "I am in rather a
difficult position. It would be very amusing
to give you a piquant account of my doings;
but I went to Borrowness of my own free will,
and even an unvarnished story of my life there
would be disloyal to my cousin. Borrowness is
not a pretty place. The country is flat, but
the coast is simply glorious. The rocks——"

"Thanks—I don't mind taking the rocks for
granted. I want to hear about your cousin and
the shop."

"I will give you a rough outline of my cousin,
and leave the details to your vivid imagination.
She is very kind, very pious, very narrow, and
very dull."

"*Good Lord deliver us!*" murmured Lucy,
gravely. "And the shop?"

"The shop is awful. You can imagine nothing
worse than the truth."

"A nice sphere for Mona Maclean!"

"Oh, my dear, there is sphere enough in all
conscience — only too much sphere! I never
saw so clearly in my life before that nothing

depends on what a man does, but that everything depends on how he does it.   Even that
twopenny - halfpenny shop might be made a
centre of culture and taste and refinement for
the whole neighbourhood."

"You would have to get rid of your cousin
first."

"I don't know.   One would rather have quite
a free hand.   But she is wonderfully liberal
about things that must seem sheer nonsense
to her."

"She well may be!"

"That is absurd.   Why should she pay in
appreciation for qualities that she does not in
the least want, and would rather be without?
You must not judge of my suitability to her
by my suitability to—you, for instance."

"Then she does not even appreciate you?"

Mona meditated before replying.   "She likes
me," she said, "but she thinks me absurdly
'superior' one minute, and gratuitously frivolous
the next.   She has not got hold of the main
thread of my character, so of course she thinks
me a bundle of inconsistencies."

"Why do you stay?"

Mona sighed.   "We won't go into that, dear.

I have committed myself. Besides, my cousin likes me; she was very unwilling to part with me, even for a week."

"Selfish brute!" said Lucy, inconsistently. "Is there any society?"

"No; but if there were, it would consider itself a cut above me."

"Any men?"

There was a momentary pause. "My dear, do I ever know anything about the men in a place?"

"I was hoping you had started a few of your Platonic friendships. They would at least save you from moping to death."

"Moping to death!" said Mona, springing to her feet. "My dear child, I never was farther from that in my life. I botanise, and once in a way I meet some of the greatest living scientists. I do the best sketches I ever did in my life, and I have developed a greater talent for millinery than you can even conceive!"

CHAPTER XXV.

A VOICE IN THE FOG.

A DENSE fog hung over the city.

Doris and Mona had spent half the day among the shops and stores, and Mona was in a glow of satisfaction. She was convinced that no human being had ever made a ten-pound note go so far before, and it was with difficulty that she could be induced to talk of anything else.

Doris was much amused. She believed in letting people "gang their ain gait," and a day with Mona was worth having under most conditions; but how any intelligent human being could elect to spend it so, was more than she could divine.

"It would have come to all the same in the end," she said, laughing, "if you had sent a general order to the Stores, and left the details to them; and it would have saved a vast amount of energy."

"Ah!" said Mona. When the two girls were together, Mona felt about petty things what Doris felt about great ones, that one must not expect absolute sympathy even from one's dearest friends.

By common consent, however, they dropped into St James's Hall for an hour, when their work was over, to refresh themselves with a little music. The overture to Tannhäuser was the last item on the programme, and Mona would have walked twenty miles any day to hear that. It was dark when they left the building, and the fog had reduced the sphere of each street lamp to a radius of two or three yards; but Mona could easily have found her way home to "blessed Bloomsbury" with her eyes shut. Doris was going to the Reynolds' to supper, to meet Lucy for the first time, and her aunt's brougham was to fetch her at night.

"Listen, Mona," she said suddenly, as they made their way along Piccadilly, "there are two men behind us discussing your beloved Tannhäuser."

This was interesting. Mona mentally relin-

quished her knick-knacks, and pricked up her
ears.

At first she could only hear something about
" sheer noise," "hideous crash of chords," "gospel
of din"; but a moment later the hand that
rested on Doris's arm twitched involuntarily, for
the mellow, cultured voice that took up the discussion was strangely familiar.

" My dear fellow, to my mind that is precisely the point of the whole thing. The Pilgrims' Chorus is beautiful and suggestive when
one hears it simply and alone, in its own special
sphere, so to speak ; but when it rises clear,
steady, and unvarying, without apparent exer-
tion, above all the reiterated noise and crash
and distraction of the world, the flesh, and the
devil,—why, then, it is an inspiration. It becomes triumphant by sheer force of continuing
to be itself."

The first voice said something about " want
of melody," and then the deep bass went
on,—

" I am not at all learned in the discussion
from a technical point of view. To my mind it
is simply a question of making the opera an
organic whole,—not a collection of works of art,

but one work of art. Take *Don Juan* for instance——"

The men turned down a side street, and the voices died away in the distance.

"What a beautiful voice!" said Doris.

"Yes."

"Do you know, Mona, I think that must have been a nice man."

"Because of the voice?"

"Because of the voice, and because of what the voice said. Young men don't talk like that as a rule."

"How do you know he was young?"

"I am sure that 'my dear fellow' was not more than twenty-five."

"Twenty-seven, I should think," said Mona, reflectively.

Doris laughed. "You are very exact. Or is it that you have gone back to the ink-stands?"

Mona sighed. "Yes," she said, gravely, "I have gone back to the inkstands."

There was silence for a few minutes.

"I should like to know who that young man was," said Doris, presently.

"Why, Doris, you are coming out in a new

rôle. It is not like you to be interested in a young man."

" The more reason why I should be interested in an exceptional one."

" You dear old Doris !" said Mona, affectionately. " He talks well, certainly ; but what if talking be, like Gretchen's beauty, his *Verderben ?* "

" I don't think it likely—not that kind of talking."

" Assuredly that kind—if any."

But she thought, " Not any. He has chosen the right corrective. If he possesses the gift of utterance, he will at least have something to utter."

" It has been such a delightful week," said Doris, "and now another nice long railway journey with you to-morrow will bring it all to an end. You are a highly privileged mortal, Mona, to be able to order your life as you choose."

Mona smiled without replying. This was a well-worn subject of debate.

" I know what you are going to say," continued Doris. " But it is no use asking me. I don't know *which* of those little inkstands was the best, and I think you did very wisely in ordering an equal number of both."

"Yes," said Mona; "and the hinges were so strong, weren't they? That is the point to look to in a cheap inkstand."

"What an age you have been!" said Lucy, as they entered the dining-room, where she was seated by the fire, arrayed in her comfortable dressing-gown. "I was just going to send the bellman after you. So glad to meet you, Miss Colquhoun."

"She is not so pretty as I am," Lucy thought, "but Mona will never see that."

Certainly Lucy's interest in the afternoon's shopping abundantly atoned for Doris's lofty indifference. "Of course, you had to have the things sent straight to the station," she said, "but I do wish I could have gone with you. Tell me all about it. Where did you go first?"

Fortunately Mr Reynolds came in at this moment, so Doris was not forced to go over all the ribbons and flowers and note-paper and what-nots again.

"Keep a thing seven years, and its use will come," said Mona. "My childish passion for

shop-windows and pretty things has stood me
in good stead, you see. You have no idea how
crisp and fresh all the things looked. The
shop will simply be another place. I need
not blush now whenever a new customer comes
in."

"How I wish I could come and see it!" said
Lucy. "I am sure I could 'dress a window'
beautifully. Do you think Borrowness would
do me as much good as the Riviera? It would
come a great deal cheaper, would not it?"

"Much," said Mona, smiling; "but the cutting
east wind has a knack of finding out one's weak
places, and you must not forget that you have
a traitor in the garrison now."

"It is so awfully unfortunate! My fees are
paid, and of course there have been a lot of
new books this term. Father simply cannot
afford to send me away."

"Don't fret. · I think you will find that it
can be done very cheaply."

"Cheapness is a relative thing. You must
remember that our whole income does not come
to much more than yours."

"Well, at least your board here would be
saved."

In point of fact, Mona had already written to Lady Munro about her friend's illness, and she hoped the answer would be an invitation to Lucy to spend a month or two at Cannes. Mona knew that the Munros were not at all the kind of people who are on the outlook for opportunities to benefit their fellow-men, but for that very reason they might be the more likely to do a graceful action that actually came in their way. The arrangement was extremely awkward, so far as she herself was concerned, for she did not mean the Munros to know that she was spending the winter at Borrowness. However, that was a minor and selfish consideration, and no doubt it could be arranged somehow.

In the midst of the conversation supper was announced. It was a homely meal, but the simplest proceedings always acquired a charm and dignity when Mr Reynolds took part in them. As soon as it was over he took Mona aside.

"Dr Bateson tells me it is very desirable that Lucy should get into a warmer climate for a month or two," he said, " before a rheumatic habit has any chance to assert itself. I am anxious to send her to the south of France, and I want you to tell me how it can be cheaply and satisfactorily done. I need not tell you, after what you saw of our life when you were with us, that Lucy's education is a heavy strain upon my purse. In fact, I give it to her because a profession is almost the only provision I can make for her future. I never allow myself to be absolutely unprepared for an unexpected drain; but Lucy's hospital fees have just been paid, and altogether this has come at a most unfortunate time."

"I know very little about the matter at present," said Mona, "but I can easily make inquiries, as I have friends in the Riviera now. My impression is, that you can do it satisfactorily, and at the same time cheaply; but I will let you know before the end of the week."

"If my aunt declines to rise to the occasion," she thought, "I will manage by hook or by crook to make them take the money from me."

Meanwhile Doris and Lucy were getting on together pretty well. Doris was shy, but she was prejudiced in Lucy's favour by the fact that she was a woman and a medical student. Lucy was not at all shy, but she was somewhat prejudiced against Doris by the fact that she was Mona's oldest friend.

" Did not Mona look lovely at Mrs Percival's 'At Home'?" asked Lucy. " She always looks nice; but in that blue velvet, with her old lace and pearls, I think she is like an empress."

" She has a very noble face, and a very lovable face. I suppose she is not beautiful, though it is not always easy to believe it."

" Was she a great success?"

" I don't think I quite know what you mean by a success. Mona never commands a room. Perhaps she might if she laid herself out to do it. Every one who spoke to her seemed much interested in her conversation."

This was scarcely to the point. What Lucy wanted to know was whether Mona had proved "fetching"; but Doris's serene face was not encouraging, and she dared not ask.

" Mona is a fortunate being," she said.

" Oh, very!"

" It must be delightful to have plenty of new gowns and all sorts of pretty things."

Doris looked aghast. Mona sometimes talked in this way, but then Mona was—Mona. No one could look at her face and suspect her of real frivolity; but this child ought to be careful.

"It must be a great deal more delightful to be able to study medicine," she said, with a little more warmth than she intended.

Lucy shrugged her shoulders. "Oh yes," she said, uncertain whether she was speaking in jest or in earnest. Then she laughed,—

> "So ist es in der Welt;
> Der Eine hat den Beutel,
> Der Andere das Geld."

"The fact is, our circles did not overlap much," she confided to Mona afterwards. "Our circumferences just touched somewhere about the middle of your circle."

"You see, Doris is a great soul."

"Ample reason, truly, why her circle should not coincide with mine. But you know, Mona, she would be a deal more satisfactory if she were a little less great, or a little small as well."

"She told me you were a dear little thing, and so pretty."

"*She's* not pretty!"

"Perhaps not, but she is fascinating, just because she never tries to fascinate. A man of the world said to me at that 'At Home,' that Miss Colquhoun was just the woman to drive a man over head and ears in love."

"Did he really ? Miss Colquhoun ? How queer ! What did you say ?"

"I cordially agreed with him."

"But has she had many offers ?"

"She would not talk of them if she had; but you may take it as broadly true, that every man of her acquaintance is either living in hope, or has practically—I say *practically*—been rejected."

"Oh, Mona, that is a large order ! You see, the fact is, I am jealous of Miss Colquhoun."

"My dear Pussy ! Doris and I were chums before you were born."

"*Raison de plus !* Look here, dear ! you say things to me that you would not say to her ?"

"Oh yes !"

"And you don't say things to her that you would not say to me ?"

"Oh yes !"

Lucy laughed, discomfited. "I choose not to believe it," she said.

Mona kissed her affectionately. "Come, that is right ! With that comfortable creed for a pillow, you ought to have an excellent night."

CHAPTER XXVI.

A CHAT BY THE FIRE.

MONA hesitated at the door of her own room, and then decided to run down for ten minutes to the sitting-room fire. She was too depressed to go to bed, and she wanted something to change the current of her thoughts. To her surprise, she found Mr Reynolds still in his large arm-chair, apparently lost in thought.

Prompted by a sudden impulse, she seated herself on a stool close to him, and laid her hand on his knee.

"Mr Reynolds," she said, "life looks very grey sometimes."

He smiled. "We all have to make up our minds to that, dear;" and after a pause he added, "This is a strange duty that you have imposed upon yourself."

" Yes."

" For six months, is it not ? "

" Yes."

" How much of the time is over ? "

" Little more than one month."

" And the life is very uncongenial ? "

" At the present moment—desperately. Not always," she added, laughing bravely. " Sometimes I feel as if the sphere were only too great a responsibility ; but now—I don't know how to face it to-morrow."

" Poor child ! I can only guess at all your motives for choosing it ; but you know that

'Tasks in hours of insight willed,
Can be through hours of gloom fulfilled.' "

" Mr Reynolds, it was not insight, it was impulse. You see, I really had worked intelligently and conscientiously for years ; I had never indulged in amusement purely for amusement's sake ; and when I failed a second time in my examination, I felt as if the stars in their courses were fighting against me. It seemed no use to try again. Things had come to a deadlock. From the time when I was little more than a child, I had had the ordering of my own

life, and perhaps you will understand how I
longed for some one to take the reins for a bit.
On every side I saw girls making light of, and
ignoring, home duties; and, just I suppose
because I had never had any, such duties had
always seemed to me the most sacred and
precious bit of moral training possible. I considered at that time that my cousin was practically my only living relative, and she was very
anxious that I should go to her. I had promised
to spend a fortnight with her in the autumn;
but the day after I knew that I had failed, I
wrote offering to stay six months.

"Of course I ought to have waited till I saw
her and the place; but her niece had just been
married, and she really wanted a companion.
If I did not go, she must look out for some one
else. I don't mean to pretend that that was my
only reason for acting impulsively. The real
reason was, that I wanted to commit myself to
something definite, to burn my boats on some
coast or other. I seemed to have muddled my
own life, and here was a human being who really
wanted me, a human being who had some sort
of natural right to me."

"Dear child, why did you not come and be

my elder daughter for a time ? It would have been a grand thing for me."

Mona laughed through her tears, and, taking his delicate white hand in both her own, she raised it to her lips. "Sir Douglas said nearly the same thing, though he does not know what I am doing ; but either of you would have spoilt me a great deal more than I had ever spoilt myself. You were kind enough to ask me to come to you at the time ; but I thought then that I had passed my examination, and I did not know you as I do now. I was restless, and wanted to shake off the cobwebs on a walking tour ; but when I heard that I had failed, all the energy seemed to go out of me."

It was some minutes before he spoke.

"Tell me about your life at Borrowness. There is a shop, is there not ? "

"I don't quarrel with the shop," said Mona, warmly ; "the shop is the redeeming feature. You don't know how it brings me in contact with all sorts of little joys and sorrows. I sometimes think I see the very selves of the women and girls, as neither priest nor Sunday-school teacher does. I have countless opportunities of sympathising, and helping, and planning, and economising—even of educating the tastes of the people, the least little bit—and of suggesting other ways of looking at things."

" And what about your cousin ? "

Mona hesitated. "I told Lucy that to give even a plain, unvarnished account of my life at Borrowness would be a disloyalty to my cousin, but one can say anything to you. Mr Reynolds, I knew before I went that my cousin was not a gentlewoman, that ours had for two generations been the successful, hers the unsuccessful, branch of my father's family. I knew she lived a simple and narrow life ; but how could I tell that my cousin would be vulgar ?—that if under any circumstances it was possible to take a mean and sordid view of a person, or an action, or a thing, she would be sure to take that mean and sordid view ? I have almost made a vow never to lose my temper, but it is hard—it is all the harder because she is so good !

" Now you know the whole story. Pitch into me well. You are the only person who is in a position to do it, so your responsibility is great."

He had never taken his eyes from her mobile face while she was speaking. "I have no wish to pitch into you well," he said; "you disarm one at every turn. I need not tell you that your action in the first instance was hasty and childish—perhaps redeemed by just a dash of heroism."

Mona lifted her face with quivering lips.

"Never mind the heroism," she said, with a rather pathetic smile. "It *was* hasty and childish."

"But I do mind the heroism very much," he said, passing his hand over her wavy brown hair. "I believe that some of the deeds which we all look upon as instances of sublime renunciation have been done in just such a spirit. It is one of the cases in which it is very difficult to tell where the noble stops and the ignoble begins. But of one thing I am quite sure—the hasty and childish spirit speedily died a natural death, and the spirit of heroism has survived to bear the burden imposed by the two."

"Don't talk of heroism in connection with me." Mona bit her lip. "I see there is one thing more that I ought to tell you, since I have told you so much. When I went to Borrowness there was some one there a great deal more cultured than myself, whose occasional society just made all the difference in my life, though I did not recognise it at the time. It is partly because I have not that to look forward to when I go back that life seems so unbearable."

"Man or woman?"

"Man, but he was nice enough to be a woman."

The words were spoken with absolute simplicity. Clearly, the idea of love and marriage had not crossed her mind.

"Did he know your circumstances?"

"No; he took for granted that Borrowness was my home. I might have told him; but my cousin had asked me not to mention the fact that I was a medical student."

"And he has gone?"

"Yes; he may be back for a week or so at Christmas, but I don't know even that." Mona looked up into the old man's face. "Now," she said, "you know the whole truth as thoroughly as I know it myself."

He repaid her look with interest.

"Honest is not the word for her," he thought. "She is simply crystalline."

"If I had the right," he said, "I should ask you to promise me one thing."

"Don't say '*If* I had the right,'" said Mona. "Claim it."

"Promise that you will not again give away your life, or any appreciable part of it, on mere impulse, without abundant consideration."

"I will promise more than that if you like. I will promise not to commit myself to anything new without first consulting you."

He could scarcely repress a smile. Evidently she did not foresee the contingency that had prompted his words. What a simple-hearted child she was, after all!

"I decline to accept that promise," he said; "I have abundant faith in your own judgment, if you only give it a hearing. But when your mind is made up, you know where to find a sympathetic ear; or if you should be in doubt or difficulty, and care to have an old man's advice, you know where to come for it. Make me the promise I asked for at first; that is all I want."

Mona looked up again with a smile, and clasped her hands on his knee. "I promise," she said, slowly, "never again to give away my life, or any appreciable part of it, on mere impulse, without abundant consideration."

He smiled down at the bright face, and then stooped to kiss her forehead. "And now," he said, "let us take the present as we find it. I suppose no one but yourself can decide whether this duty is the more or the less binding because it is self-imposed."

Mona's face expressed much surprise. "Oh," she said, "I have not the smallest doubt on that score. I must go through with it now that I have put my hand to the plough."

"I am glad you think so, though there is something to be said on the other side as well. Your mind is made up, and that being so, you don't need me to tell you that you are doubly bound to take the life bravely and brightly, because you have chosen it yourself. Fortunately, yours is a nature that will develop in any surroundings. But I do want to say a word or two about your examination, and the life you have thrown aside for the time. I know you don't talk about it, but I think you will allow me to say what I feel. Preaching, you know, is an old man's privilege."

"Go on," said Mona, "talk to me. Nobody helps me but you. It does me good even to hear your voice."

CHAPTER XXVII.

A NEOPHYTE.

ONCE more Mona arrived at Borrowness, and once more Rachel was awaiting her at the station.

There was no illusion now about the life before her, no uncertainty, no vague visions of self-renunciation and of a vocation. All was flat, plain, shadowless prose.

"I must e'en dree my weird," she said to herself as the train drew into the station; but a bright face smiled at Rachel from the carriage-window, a light step sprang on to the platform, and a cheerful voice said—

"Well, you see I am all but true to my word; and you have no idea what a lot of pretty things I have brought with me."

"Mona," said Rachel, mysteriously, as they

walked down the road to the house, "I have a piece of news for you. Who do you think called?"

"I am afraid I can't guess."

"Mr Brown!"

"Did he?" said Mona, rather absently.

"Yes. At first I was that put out at you being away, and I had the awfullest hurry getting on my best dress; but just as I was showing him out, who should pass but Mrs Robertson. My word, didn't she stare! The Browns would never think of calling on her. I told him you were away visiting friends. I didn't say in London, for fear he might find out about your meaning to be a doctor."

"That would be dreadful, would not it?"

"Yes, but you needn't be afraid. He said something about its being a nice change for you to come here after teaching, and I never let on you weren't a teacher, though it was on the tip of my tongue to tell him what a nice bit of a tocher you had of your own."

"Pray don't say that to any one," said Mona, rather sharply. "I have no wish to be buzzed round by a lot of raw Lubins in search of Phyllis with a tocher."

" Well, my dear, you know you're getting on. It's best to make hay while the sun shines."

" True," said Mona, cynically ; " but when a woman has even three hundred a-year of her own, she has a good long day before her."

Early in the evening Bill arrived with Mona's boxes, and the two cousins entered with equal zest upon the work of unpacking them. " My word ! " and " Well, I never ! " fell alternately from Rachel's lips as treasure after treasure came to view. Ten pounds was a great sum of money, to be sure ; but who would have thought that even ten pounds could buy all this ? " You *are* a born shopkeeper, Mona ! " she said, with genuine admiration.

Mona laughed. " Shall we advertise in the *Gazette* that ' Our Miss Maclean has just returned from a visit to London, and has brought with her a choice selection of all the novelties of the season ' ? " she said ; but she withdrew the suggestion hastily, when she saw that Rachel was disposed to take it seriously.

" And now," she went on, " there is one thing more, not for the shop but for you ; " and from shrouding sheets of tissue-paper, she unfolded a quiet, handsome fur-lined cloak.

"Oh, my goodness!" Rachel had never seen anything so magnificent in her life, and the tears stood in her eyes as she tried it on.

"It's your kindness I'm thinking of, my dear, not of the cloak," she said; "but there isn't the like of it between this and St Rules. It'll last me all my life."

Mona kissed her on the forehead, well pleased.

"And I brought a plain muff and tippet for Sally. She says she always has a cold in the winter. This is a reward to her for spending some of her wages on winter flannels, sorely against her will."

"Dear me! She will be set up. There will be no keeping her away from Bible Class and Prayer Meeting now! It is nice having you back, Mona. I can't tell you how many folk have been asking for you in the shop; there's twice as much custom since you came. Miss Moir wouldn't buy a hat till you came back to help her to choose it; and Polly Baines from the Towers brought in some patterns of cloth to ask your advice about a dress."

"Did she? How sweet of her! I hope you

told her to call again. Has the Colonel's Jenny been in ?"

"Oh no, it's very seldom she gets this length. Kirkstoun's nearer, and there's better shops."

"She told me there's no one to write her letters for her, since Maggie went away, and I promised to go out there before long and act the part of scribe. It was quite a weight on my mind while I was in London, but I will go as soon as I get these things arranged in the shop. Has the Colonel gone yet?"

"No; I understand he goes to his sisters to-morrow."

Most of Jenny's acquaintances gladly seized the opportunity to call on her when her master was away from home. The Colonel had the reputation of being the most outrageously eccentric man in the whole country-side, and it required courage of no common order to risk an accidental encounter with him. He might chance, of course, to be in an extremely affable humour, but it was impossible to make sure of this beforehand; and one thing was quite certain, that the natural frankness of his intercourse with his fellow-men was not likely to be modified by any sense of tact, or even of common decency. What he thought he said, and he often delighted in saying something worse than his deliberate thought. Not many years before, his family had owned the whole of the estate on which he was now content to rent a pretty cottage, standing some miles from the sea, in a few acres of pine-wood. Here he lived for a great part of the year, alone with his quaint old housekeeper Jenny, taking no part in the social life of the neighbourhood, but calling on whom he chose, when he chose, regardless of all etiquette in the matter. Strange tales were told of him—tales to which Jenny listened in sphinx-like silence, never giving wing to a bit of gossip by so much as an " Ay " or "Nay." She had grown thoroughly accustomed to the old man's ways, and it seemed to be nothing to her if his language was as strong as his potions.

"Have a glass of whisky and water, Colonel ? " Mrs Hamilton had asked one cold morning, when he dropped into her house soon after breakfast.

"Thank you, madam," he had replied, " I won't trouble you for the water."

The clever old lady was a prime favourite

with him, the more so as she considered it the prescriptive right of a soldier of good family to be as outrageous as he chose.

He was a kind-hearted man, too, and fond of children, though they rarely lost their fear of him. He was reported to be " unco near," but if he met a bright-faced child whom he knew, in his favourite resort, the post-office, he would say—

" Sixpenn'orth of sweets for this young lady, Mr Dalgleish. You may put in as many more as you like from yourself, but sixpenn-'orth will be from me."

Mona was somewhat curious to see the old man, as she fancied that in her childhood she had heard her father speak of him; but her time was fully occupied in the shop for some days after her return. Rachel had actually con-sented to have the old place re-papered and painted, and when Mona put the finishing touch to her arrangements one afternoon, no one would have recognised " Miss Simpson's shop."

Mona clapped her hands in triumph, and feasted her eyes on the work of reformation. Then she looked at her watch, but it was already late, and as the Colonel's wood lay three or four miles off, her visit had to be postponed once more. She was too tired to sketch, so she took a book and strolled down to Castle Maclean.

It was a quiet, grey afternoon. The distant hills were blotted out, but the rocky coast was as grand as ever, and the plash of the waves, as they broke on the beach beneath her, was sweeter in her ears than music.

She was disturbed in her reverie by a step on the rocks, and for a moment her heart beat quicker. Then she almost laughed at her own stupidity. And well she might, for the step only heralded the approach of Matilda Cookson, with her smart hat and luxuriant red hair.

"Where ever have you been, Miss Maclean?" she began rather breathlessly, seating herself on a ledge of rock. "I have been looking out for a chance of speaking to you for nearly a fortnight."

Mona's face expressed the surprise she felt.

"I have been away from home," she said. "What did you want with me?"

"Away from home! Then you haven't told anybody yet?"

Mona began to think that one or other of

them must be the victim of delusional insanity.

"Told anybody—*what?*"

Matilda frowned. If Miss Maclean had really noticed nothing, it was a pity she had gone out of her way to broach the subject, but she could not withdraw from it now.

"I thought you saw me—that day at St Rules."

"*Oh!*" said Mona, as the recollection came slowly back to her. "So I did,—but why do you wish me not to tell any one?"

Matilda blushed violently at the direct question, and proceeded to draw designs on the carpet of Castle Maclean with the end of her umbrella. She had intended to dispose of the matter in a few airy words; and she felt convinced still that she could have done so in her own house, or in Miss Simpson's shop, if she had chanced to see Miss Maclean alone in either place. But Mona looked so serenely and provokingly at home out here on the rocks, with the half-cut German book in her delicate white hands, that the whole affair began to assume a much more serious aspect.

Mona studied the crimson face attentively.

It had been her strong instinctive impulse to say, " My dear child, if you had not reminded me of it I should never have thought of the matter again," and so to dismiss the subject. But she was restrained from doing so by a vague recollection of her conversation with Dr Dudley about these girls. She forgot that she was supposed to be their social inferior, and remembered only that she was a woman, responsible in a greater or a less degree for every girl with whom she came in contact.

She laid her hand on her visitor's shoulder.

" You may be quite sure," she said, " that I don't want to get you into trouble, but I think you had better tell me why you wish me not to speak of this."

Mona's touch was mesmeric,—at least Matilda Cookson found it so. In all her vapid little life she had never experienced anything like the thrill that passed through her now. She would have confessed anything at that moment, and perhaps have regretted her frankness bitterly an hour later; for, after all, confession is only occasionally of moral value in itself, however priceless it may be in its results.

The story was not a particularly novel one,

even to Mona's inexperienced ears. Two years before, all the girls in Miss Barnett's private school at Kirkstoun had been "in love" with the drawing-master, who came twice a-week from St Rules. His languid manner and large dark eyes had wrought havoc within the "narrowing nunnery walls," and when his work at St Rules had increased so much that he no longer required Miss Barnett's support, he had taken his departure amid much wailing and lamentation.

Matilda had gone soon after to a London boarding-school, where she had forgotten all about him ; but a chance meeting at a dance, on her return, had renewed the old attraction. This first chance meeting had been followed by a number of others ; and when, only a short time before, Mrs Cookson had suddenly decreed that Matilda was to go to St Rules once a-week for music lessons, the temptation to create a few more " chance meetings " had proved irresistible.

Mona was rather at a loss to know what to do with the confession, now that she had got it. She knew so little of this girl. What were her gods? Had she any heroes?—any heroines?

—any ideals? Was there anything in her to which one might appeal? Mona was too young herself to attack the situation with weapons less cumbrous than heavy artillery.

"How old are you?" she asked, suddenly.

"Eighteen."

"And don't you mean to be a fine woman—morally a fine woman, I mean?"

"Morally a fine woman"—the words, spoken half shyly, half wistfully, were almost an unknown tongue to Matilda Cookson. Almost, but not quite. They called up vague visions of evening services, and of undefined longings for better things,—visions, more distinct, of a certain "revival," when she had become "hysterical," had stayed to the "inquiry meeting," and had professed to be "converted." She had been very happy then for a few weeks, but the happiness had not lasted long. Those things never did last; they were all pure excitement, as her father had said at the time. What was the use of raking up that old story now?

"I don't see that there was any great harm in my meeting him," she said, doggedly.

"I am quite sure you did not mean any great harm; but do you know how men talk about girls who 'give themselves away,' as they call it ? "

Matilda coloured. " I am sure he would not say anything horrid about me. He is awfully in love."

" Is he ? I don't know much about love ; but if he loves you, you surely want him to respect you. You would not like him to be a worse man for loving you,—and he must become a worse man, if he has a low opinion of women."

" You mean that I am not to meet him any more ? "

" I mean that he cannot possibly respect you, while he knows you meet him without your mother's knowledge."

" And suppose I won't promise not to meet him again, what will you do ? "

" I don't consider that I have the smallest right to exact a promise from you."

" Then you won't speak of this to any one, whatever happens ? "

Mona smiled. " I am not quite clear that you have any right to exact a promise from me."

Matilda could not help joining in the smile. This was good fencing.

" At any rate, you have not told any one yet ? "

" I have not."

" Not Miss Simpson ? "

" Not any one ; and therefore not Miss Simpson."

" Well, I must say it was very kind of you."

" I am afraid I ought not to accept your praise ; it never occurred to me to speak of it."

" And yet you recognised me ? "

Mona laughed outright — a very friendly laugh.

" And yet I recognised you."

Matilda drew the sole of her high-heeled shoe over the ground in front of her, and began an entirely new design.

" What do you mean by 'respect,' Miss Maclean ? It is such a chilly word. There is no warmth or colour in it."

" There is no warmth nor colour in the air, yet air is even more essential than sunshine."

There was silence for some minutes. Matilda obliterated the new design with a little stamp of her foot.

" Long ago, when I was a girl, I began to

believe in self-denial, and high ideals, and all
that sort of thing. But you can't work it in
with your everyday life. It is all a dream."

"A dream!" said Mona, softly,—

"'No, no, by all the martyrs and the dear dead Christ!'

Everything else is a dream. That is real.
That was your chance in life. You should have
clung to it with both hands. Your soul is
drowning now for want of it, in a sea of noth-
ingness."

The revival preacher himself could scarcely
have spoken more strongly, and Matilda felt a
slight pleasurable return of the old excitement.
She did not show it, however.

"It is easy to talk," she said, "but you don't
know what it is to be the richest people in a
place like this. Pa and Ma won't let anybody
speak to us. I believe it will end in our never
getting married at all. We shall be out of the
wood before they find their straight stick."

"My dear child, is marriage the end of life?
And even if it is, surely the girls who make
good wives are those who are content to be the
life and brightness of their home circle, and
who are not constantly straining their eyes in

search of the knight - errant who is to deliver them from Giant Irksome."

In the course of her life in London, Mona had met many girls who chafed at home duties, and longed for a 'sphere,' but a girl who longed for a husband, *quâ* husband, was so surprising an instance of atavism as to be practically a new type.

Matilda sighed. "You don't know what our home life is," she said. "We pay calls, and people call on us; we go for proper walks along the highroad; we play on the piano and we do crewel-work; we get novels from the library,— and that is all. Just the same thing over and over again."

"And don't you care enough for books and music to find scope in them?"

Matilda shook her head. "Can you read German?" she asked abruptly, looking at Mona's book.

"Yes; do you?"

"No; and I never in my life met any one who could, unless perhaps my German teachers. I took it for three years at school, but I should not know one word in ten now. I wish I did! We had a nice row, I can tell you, when I first came home from school, and Father brought in a German letter from the office one day. He actually expected me to be able to read it!"

"You could easily learn. It only wants a little dogged resolution, — enough to worry steadily through one German story-book with a dictionary. After that the neck of the difficulty is broken."

Matilda made a grimace. "I have only got *Bilderbuch*," she said, "and I know the English of that by heart, from hearing the girls go over and over it in class. Start me off, and I can go on; but I can scarcely tell you which word stands for moon."

She was almost startled at her own frankness. She had never talked like this to any one before.

"You know I am not going to take you at your own valuation. Let me judge for myself," and Mona opened her book at the first page and held it out.

Matilda put her hands up to her face. "*Don't!*" she said. "I couldn't bear to let you see how little I know. But I will try to learn. I will begin *Bilderbuch* this very night, though I hate it as much as I do *Lycidas* and *Hamlet*, and everything else I read at school."

Mona shivered involuntarily. "Don't read anything you are sick of," she said. "If you like, I will lend you an interesting story that will tempt you on in spite of yourself."

"Thanks awfully. You are very kind."

"I shall be very glad to help you if you get into a real difficulty." Mona paused. "As I said before, I have no right to exact a promise from you—but I can't tell you how much more highly I should think of you if you did worry on to the end."

The conclusion of this sentence took Matilda by surprise. She had imagined that Mona was going back to the subject of the drawing-master, but Mona seemed to have forgotten the existence of everything but German books.

"And may I come here sometimes in the afternoon, and talk to you? I often see you go down to the beach."

"I never know beforehand when I shall be able to come; but, if you care to take the chance, I shall always be glad to see you."

"The new Adam will," she said to herself,

with a half-amused, half-rueful smile, when her visitor had gone, " but the old Adam will have a tussle for his rights."

A moment later Matilda reappeared, shy and awkward.

" Would you mind telling me again that thing you said about the martyrs ? "

Mona smiled. " If you wait a moment, I will write it down for you ; " and, tearing a leaf from her note-book, she wrote out the whole verse—

" No, no, by all the martyrs and the dear dead Christ ;
By the long bright roll of those whom joy enticed
With her myriad blandishments, but could not win,
Who would fight for victory, but would not sin."

Matilda read it through, and then carefully folded the paper. In doing so she noticed some writing on the back and read aloud—

" Lady Munro, Poste Restante, Cannes." " Who is Lady Munro ? " she asked, with unintentional rudeness.

" She is my aunt. I did not know her address was written there." Mona tore off the name, and handed back the slip of paper.

" Lady Munro your aunt, and you live with Miss Simpson ? "

"Why not? Miss Simpson is my cousin."

"Miss Maclean, if I had a 'Lady' for my aunt, everybody should know it. I don't believe I should even travel in a railway carriage, without the other passengers finding it out."

Mona laughed. "I have already told you that I don't mean to take you at your own valuation. In point of fact, I had much rather the people here knew nothing about Lady Munro. I should not like others to draw comparisons between her and Miss Simpson."

"I beg your pardon. I did not mean——"

"Oh, I know you did not mean any harm. It was my own stupidity; but, as I say, I should not like others to talk of it. *Auf Wiederschen!*"

Alone once more, Mona clasped her hands behind her head, and looked out over the sea.

"Well, playfellow," she said, "have I done good or harm? At the present moment, as she walks home, she does not know whether to venerate or to detest me. It is an even chance which way the scale will turn. And is it all an affair of infinite importance, or does it not matter one whit?"

This estimate of Matilda's state of mind was

a shrewd one, except for one neglected item.
Now that the moment of impulse was over,
the balance might have been even; but Lady
Munro's name had turned the scale, and
Matilda 'venerated' her new friend. Mona's
strong and vivid personality would have made
any one forget in her presence that she was
'only a shop-girl'; but no power on earth
could prevent the recollection from returning—
perhaps with renewed force—when her immediate
influence was withdrawn. If a man of culture
like Dr Dudley could not wholly ignore the
fact of her social inferiority, how much less was
it possible to an empty little soul like Matilda
Cookson? for she was one of those people to
whose moral and spiritual progress an earthly
crutch is absolutely essential. She never forgot
that conversation at Castle Maclean; but the
two things that in after-years stood out most
clearly in her memory were the quotation about
the martyrs, and Mona's relationship to Lady
Munro. And surely this is not so strange?
Do not even the best of us stand with one
foot on the eternal rock, and the other on the
shifting sands of time?

"How odd that she should be struck by that

quotation!" mused Mona. "I wonder what Dr Dudley would say if he knew that the notes of the Pilgrims' Chorus, rising clear, steady, and unvarying above all the noises of the world, appealed even to the stupid little ears of Matilda Cookson. If the mother is no more than he says, there must be some good stuff in the father. *Ex nihilo, nihil fit.*"

CHAPTER XXVIII.

THE COLONEL'S YARN.

THE next morning brought Mona a budget of letters on the subject of Lucy's visit to the Riviera. Lady Munro had risen to the occasion magnificently. "If your friend is in the least like you," she wrote, "I shall be only too glad to have her as a companion for Evelyn. I have written to ask her to be my guest for a month, and the sooner she comes the better."

"I have only known you for a few years," wrote Lucy, "and I seem to have grown tired of saying that I don't know how to thank you. It will be nuts for me to go to Cannes, without feeling that my father is living on hasty-pudding at home; and it will be a great thing to be with people like the Munros; but if they expect that I am going to live up to your level, I shall simply give up the ghost at once. I have written to assure them that I am an utter and unmitigated fraud; but do you tell them the same, in case there should be bloodshed on my arrival.

"As for your dear letter and enclosure, I handed them straight over to Father, and asked him what I was to do. He read the letter twice through carefully, and then gave me back—the bank-note only! 'Keep it,' he said, briefly; and I fancied—I say I *fancied*—that there was a suspicious dimness about his eyes. You have indeed made straight tracks for the Pater's heart, Mistress Mona, if he allows his daughter to accept twenty pounds from you.

"Allowing for all the expenses of the journey, I find I can afford two gowns and a hat, and much anxious thought the selection has given me, I assure you. One thing I have absolutely settled on,—a pale sea-green Liberty silk, with suggestions of foam; and when I decided on that, I came simultaneously to another decision, that life is worth living after all.

"I only wish I felt perfectly sure that you could afford it, darling. You told me you were getting nothing new for yourself this winter, &c., &c."

Finally, there was a little note from Mr Reynolds to his "elder daughter," — a note in no way remarkable for originality, yet full of that personal, life-giving influence which is worth a thousand brilliant aphorisms.

Mona was very busy in the shop that morning, but in her spare minutes she contrived to write a letter to Lucy.

"I do not wish to put you in an awkward position," she wrote, "but I think you have sufficient ingenuity and resource to keep me out of difficulties also. You know that when I promised to go to my cousin, I had not even seen the Munros. I met them immediately afterwards; and our intimacy has ripened so rapidly that I should not now think it right to take an important step in life without at least letting them know. I mean to tell them ultimately about my winter in Borrowness; but nothing they could say would alter my opinion of my obligation to remain here, and I think I am justified in wishing to avoid useless friction in the meantime. You can imagine what the situation would be, if Sir Douglas were to

appear in the shop some fine morning, and
demand my instant return to civilised life.   He
is quite capable of doing it, and I am very
anxious if possible to avoid such a clumsy *dénouement.*   You will see at a glance how in-
artistic it would be.

"You will tell me that it is absolutely impossible to conceal the truth, but I do not think
you will find it so when you get to Cannes.   It
is very doubtful whether you will see Sir Douglas
at all,—he is looking forward so much to the
pheasant-shooting; and Lady Munro is not the
person to ask questions except in a general sort
of way.   She exists far too gracefully for that.
You can honestly say, if needful, that I am very
busy, but that I have not yet returned to town ;
I don't think you will find it necessary to say
even that.

"But show me up a thousand times over
rather than sail nearer the wind than your conscience approves.   I merely state the position,
and I know you will appreciate my difficulty
quite as fully as I do myself.

"Please don't have the smallest scruple about
accepting the money.   When I told you I was
'on the rocks,' I did not mean it in the sense in

which a young man about town would use the
expression. My debts did not amount to more
than twenty or thirty pounds. All things in
life are relative, you see. I spent nothing in
Norway, and my cousin will not hear of my
paying for my board here. She is kind enough
to say that, even pecuniarily, she is richer since
I came. Of course I do not want any more
gowns; I go nowhere, and see no one. Doris
tells me she is studying medicine—by proxy.
I am glad to think that I shall be shining in
society this winter—also by proxy. I hope I
may have the good fortune to see you in your
new *rôle* of mermaid before the run is over. I
am sure it will be a very successful one.

"Please give your father my most dutiful
love, and tell him that I will answer his kind
note in a day or two."

The writing of this letter, together with a few
grateful lines to Lady Munro, occupied all
Mona's spare time before dinner; and as soon as
the unbeautiful meal was over, she set off at last
to the Colonel's wood.

"If the scale has turned against me, Matilda
Cookson will not go to Castle Maclean," she
reflected. "If it has turned in my favour,

it will do her no harm to look for me in
vain."

She had to walk in to Kirkstoun, and then
strike up country for two or three miles; but
before she had proceeded far on her way, she
met Mr Brown.

"So you have got back," he said, looking very
shy and uncomfortable.

"Yes, I have been back for some days."

"How is Miss Simpson?"

"She is very well, thank you."

"Were you going anywhere in particular?"

"I am going to Barntoun Wood, but don't let
me take you out of your way," she said.

He did not answer, but walked by her side
into town.

"Do you take ill with the smell of tobacco?"
he asked, taking his pipe from his pocket.

"Not in the least."

"Have you been doing any more botanising?"

"I have not had time. Thank you so much
for sending me that box of treasures. Some of
them interested me greatly."

"I thought you would like them. Will you
be able to come again some day, and hunt for
yourself?"

"Is not it getting too late in the year?"

"Not for the mosses and lichens and sea-weeds. Have you gone into them at all?"

"Not a bit. They must be extremely interesting, but very difficult."

"Oh, you get hold of the thread in time, especially with the mosses. The Algæ and Fungi are a tremendous subject of course. One can only work a bit on the borders of it. But if you care to come for a few more rambles, I could soon show you the commonest things we have, and a few of the rarer ones."

"I should like it immensely. Could your sister come with us?"

"Oh yes; she was not really tired that day. It was just that her boot was too tight. I had a laugh at her when we got home."

"Well, I suppose we part company here. I am going out to Colonel Lawrence's."

"I am not doing anything particular this afternoon. I could walk out with you."

The words were commonplace, but something in his manner startled Mona.

As regarded the gift of utterance, Mr Brown was not many degrees removed from the dumb creation. He could discuss a cashmere with the

traveller, a right-of-way with a fellow-townsman,
or a bit of local gossip with his sisters. He
could talk botany to a clever young woman, and
he could blurt out in honest English the fact
that he wanted her to be his wife ; but of love-
making as an art, of the delicate *crescendo* by
which women are won in spite of themselves, he
was as ignorant as a child. It was natural and
easy to his mind to make one giant stride from
botany to marriage ; and it never occurred to
him that the woman might require a few of
those stepping-stones which developing passion
usually creates for the lover, and which *savoir
vivre* teaches the man of the world to place
deliberately.

"Thank you very much," said Mona ; "but
I could not think of troubling you. I am well
used to going about alone." She held out her
hand, but, as he did not immediately take it,
she bowed cordially, and left him helplessly
watching her retreating figure.

She passed the museum, and, leaving the
town behind her, walked out among the fields.
Most of the corn had been gathered in, but a
few stooks still remained here and there to break
the monotony of the stubble-grown acres. Trees

in that district were so rare that one scraggy
sycamore by the roadside had been christened
Balmarnie Tree, and served as an important
landmark ; while, for many miles around, the
Colonel's tiny wood stood out as a feature of
the landscape, the little freestone cottage peep-
ing from beneath the dark shade of the pines
like a rabbit from its burrow.

"It seems to me, my dear," she said to herself, "that you are rather a goose. Are you
only seventeen, may I ask, that you should be
alarmed by a conversation from Ollendorf? But
all the same, if Miss Brown's shoe pinches her
next time, my shoe shall pinch me too."

She passed Wester and Easter Barntoun, the
two large farms that constituted the greater part
of the estate ; and then a quarter of an hour's
walk brought her to Barntoun Wood. A few
small cottar-houses stood within a stone's-throw
of the gate, but the place seemed curiously
lonely to be the chosen home of an old man of
the world. Yet there could be no doubt that it
was a gentleman's residence. A well-trained
beech hedge surmounted the low stone dyke,
from whose moss-grown crannies sprang a forest
of polypody, and a few graceful fronds of wild

maidenhair. The carriage-drive was smooth and well kept, but, on leaving it, one plunged at once into the shade of the trees, with generations of pine-needles under foot, and the weird cooing of wood-pigeons above one's head. Mona longed to explore those mysterious recesses, but there was no time for that to-day. She walked straight up to the house and knocked.

She was met in the doorway by the quaintest old man she had ever beheld. His clean-shaven face was a network of wrinkles, and he wore a nut-brown wig surmounted by a red night-cap.

"Who are you?" he asked, abruptly.

"I am Mona Maclean." Some curious impulse prompted her to add, for the first time during her stay at Borrowness, not "Miss Simpson's cousin," but, "Gordon Maclean's daughter."

He seized her almost roughly by the shoulder, and turned her face to the light.

"By Gad, so you are!" he exclaimed, "though you are not so bonny as your mother was before you. But come in, come in; and tell me all about it."

He opened the door of an old-fashioned, smoke-seasoned parlour, and Mona went in.

"But I did not mean to disturb you," she said. "I came to see Jenny."

"Tut, tut, sit down, sit down! Jenny, damn ye, come and put a spunk to this fire. There's a young lady here."

The old woman came in, bobbing to Mona as she passed. She was not at all surprised to see Miss Simpson's assistant in her master's parlour. One of Jenny's chief qualifications for her post of housekeeper was the fact that she had long ceased to speculate about the Colonel's vagaries.

"I wonder what I have got that I can offer you?" said the old man, meditatively. He unlocked a small sideboard, produced from it some rather mouldy sweet biscuits, and poured out a glass of wine.

"That's lady's wine," he said, "so you need not be afraid of it. It's not what I drink myself." He laughed, and, helping himself to a small glass of whisky, he looked across at his visitor.

"Here's to old times and Gordon Maclean!" he said, "the finest fellow that ever kept open house at Rangoon," and he tossed off the whisky at a gulp.

Mona drank the toast, and smiled through a

sudden and blinding mist of tears. It was meat
and drink to her to hear her father's praise even
on lips like these.

"Come, come, don't fret," said the Colonel,
kindly. "He was a fine fellow, as I say, but I
think he knew the way to heaven all the same."

"I am quite sure of that."

"That's right, that's right. Where are you
stopping—the Towers?—Balnamora?"

"No, no; I am staying at Borrowness, with
my cousin Miss Simpson."

He stared at her blankly.

"Miss Simpson?" he said, "Rachel Simpson!" His jaw dropped, and, throwing back
his head on the top of his chair, he burst into
an unpleasant laugh.

"Your father was a rich man, though he died
young," he said, recovering himself suddenly.
"He must have left you a tidy little portion."

"So he did," said Mona. "Things were sadly
mismanaged after his death; but in the end I
got what was quite sufficient for me."

"You have had a good education?—learned to
sing, and parley-voo, and"—he ran his fingers
awkwardly up and down the table—"this sort
of thing?"

Mona laughed. "Yes," she said, "I have learned all that."

He puffed away at his pipe for a time in silence.

"Why are you not with the Munros?" he said, abruptly. "With Munro's eye for a pretty young woman, too!"

"The Munros took me to Norway this summer. Sir Douglas is kindness itself, and so is Lady Munro; but Miss Simpson is my cousin."

He laughed again, the same discordant laugh.

"Drink your wine, Miss Maclean," he said, "and I will spin you a bit of a yarn. Maybe some of it will be news to you.

"A great many years before you were born, my grandfather was the laird of all this property. Your father's people, the Macleans, were tenants on the estate—respectable, well-to-do tenants, in a small way. Your grandfather was a remarkable man, cut out for success from his cradle,—always at the top of his class at school, don't you know? always keen to know what made the wheels go round, always ready to touch his hat to the ladies. His only brother, Sandy, was a ne'er-do-weel who never came to anything, but your grandfather soon became a rich man. There were two sisters, and each took after one of the brothers, so to say. Margaret was a fine, strapping, fair-spoken wench; Ann was a poor fusionless thing, who married the first man that asked her. Margaret never married. The best grain often stands.

"Your grandfather had, let me see, three children—two boys and a girl. A boy and girl died. It was a sad story — you'll know all about it? — fine healthy children, too! But your father was a chip of the old block. He had a first-rate education, and then he went to India and made a great name for himself. I never knew a man like him. People opened their hearts and homes to him wherever he went. Not a door that was closed to him, and yet he never forgot an old friend. Well, the first time he came home, like the gentleman he was, he must needs look up his people here. Most of them were dead. Sandy had gone to Australia; there were only Ann's children, Rachel Simpson and her sister Jane. Jane had married a small shopkeeper, and had a boy and girl of her own. They were very poor, so he made each of them a yearly allowance.

" Well, he was visiting with his young wife

at a house not a hundred miles from here, and the two of them were the life of the party. I know all about it, because I came to stay at the house myself a day or two before they left. After they had gone — *after they had gone*, mark ye!—who should come to call at the house in all their war-paint but Rachel Simpson and her sister! And, by Jove! they were a queerish couple. Rachel had notions of her own about dress in those days, I can tell you."

Mona blushed crimson. No one who knew Rachel could have much doubt that the story was true.

"They announced themselves as 'Gordon Maclean's cousins,' and of course they were civilly received; but the footman got orders that if they called again his mistress was not at home. I had a pretty good inkling that Maclean was providing them with funds, so I thought it only right to tip him a wink. He took it amazingly well—he *was* a good fellow! —but I believe he gave his fair cousins pretty plainly to understand that, though he was willing to share his money, his friends were his own till he chose to introduce them. I never heard of their playing that little game again, for, after all, the funds were of even more importance than the high connections. But they never forgave your father. They always thought that he might have pulled them up the ladder with him—ha, ha, ha! a pretty fair weight they would have been!"

Mona did not laugh. Nothing could make the least difference now, but she did wish she had heard this story before.

"You did not know old Simpy in your father's time?"

Mona hesitated. She was half inclined to resent the insulting diminutive, but what was the use? The Colonel took liberties with every one, and perhaps he could tell her more.

"No," she said. "I vaguely knew that I had a cousin, but I never thought much about it till she wrote to me a few years ago."

"The deuce she did! To borrow money, I'll be bound. That nephew of hers was a regular sink for money, till he and his mother died. But Simpy should be quite a millionaire now. She has the income your father settled on her, and a little money besides—let alone the shop! She is not sponging on you now, I hope?"

"Oh no," said Mona, warmly. "On the contrary, I am staying here as her guest."

He burst out laughing again.

"Rather you than me!" he said. "But well you may; it is all your father's money, first or last."

Mona rose to go.

"I am glad you have told me all this," she said, "though it is rather depressing."

"Depressing? Hoot, havers! It will teach you how to treat Rachel Simpson for the future. I have a likeness of your father and mother here. Would you like to see it?"

"Very much indeed. It may be one I have never seen."

He took up a shabby old album, and turned his back while he found the place; but a page must have slipped over by accident in his shaky old hands, for when Mona looked she beheld only a vision of long white legs and flying gauzy petticoats.

"Damnation!" shouted the old man, and snatching the book away, he hastily corrected his mistake.

It was all right this time. No living faces were so familiar to Mona as were those of the earnest, capable man, and the beautiful, queenly woman in the photograph.

" I have never seen this before," she said. " It is very good."

" I'll leave it to you in my will, eh? It will be worth as much as most of my legacies."

"If everything you leave is as much valued as that will be, your legatees will have much to be grateful for."

The old face furrowed up into a broad smile. " Well," he said, " I start for London to-night, but I hope we may meet again. I'll send Jenny in to see you. We are good comrades, she and I—we never inquire into each other's affairs."

Mona found it rather difficult to give her full attention to Jenny's letters, interesting and characteristic as these were. One was addressed to a sailor brother; another to Maggie, and the latter was not at all unlike a quaint paraphrase of Polonius's advice to his son. The poor woman's mind was apparently ill at ease about the child of her old age.

" I suld hae keepit her by me," she said. " She's ower young tae fend for hersel'; but it was a guid place, an' she was that keen tae gang, puir bit thing!"

"I do think it would be well if you could get her a good place somewhere in the neighbourhood," said Mona; "and I should not think it would be difficult."

"Ay, but she maun bide her year. It's an ill beginning tae shift ere the twel'month's oot. We maun e'en thole."

But Jenny forgot her forebodings in her admiration of Mona's handwriting.

"I can maist read it mysel'," she said. "Ye write lood oot, like the print i' the big Bible."

CHAPTER XXIX.

"YONDER SHINING LIGHT."

MISS SIMPSON's shop had undeniably become one of the lions of Borrowness. An advertisement in the *Kirkstoun Gazette* would have been absolutely useless, compared with the rumour which ran from mouth to mouth, and which brought women of all classes to see the novelties for themselves. Rachel had to double and treble her orders when the traveller came round, and it soon became quite impossible for her and Mona to leave the shop at the same time.

"I find it a little difficult to do as you asked me about reading," Mona wrote to Mr Reynolds, "for the shop-keeping really has become hard work, calling for all one's resources; and my cousin naturally expects me to be sociable

for a couple of hours in the evening. I keenly
appreciate, however, what you said about beginning the work leisurely, and leaving a minimum
of strain to the end; so I make it a positive
duty to read for one hour a-day, and, as a
general rule, the hour runs on to two. When
my six months here are over, I will take a short
holiday, and then put myself into a regular
tread-mill till July; and I will do my very best
to pass. What you said to me that night is
perfectly true. I have read too much *con
amore*, going as far afield as my fancy led me,
and neglecting the old principle of 'line upon
line; precept upon precept.' It certainly has
been my experience, that *wisdom* comes, but
knowledge lingers; and I mean this time, as a
Glasgow professor says, to stick to a policy of
limited liability, and learn nothing that will not
pay. That is what the examiners want, and
they shall not have to tell me so a third time!

" Forgive this bit of pique. It is an expiring
flame. I don't really cherish one atom of resentment in my heart. I admit that I was
honestly beaten by the rules of the game; and,
from the point of view of the vanquished, there
is nothing more to be said. I will try to leave

no more loose ends in my life, if I can help it,
and I assure you my resolution in this respect
is being subjected to a somewhat stern test here.

"It was very wise and very kind of you to
make me talk the whole subject out. I should
not be so hard and priggish as I am, if, like
Lucy, I had had a father."

One morning when Rachel was out, three
elderly ladies entered the shop. They were
short, thick-set, sedate, unobtrusively dignified,
and at a first glance they all looked exactly
alike. At a second glance, however, certain
minor points of difference became apparent.
One had black cannon-curls on each side of her
face; one wore an eyeglass; and the third was
easily differentiated by the total absence of all
means of differentiation.

"I hear Miss Simpson has got a remarkable
collection of new things," said the one with the
curls.

"Not at all remarkable, I fear," said Mona,
smiling. "But she has got a number of fresh
things from London. If you will sit down, I
will show you anything you care to see."

If Mona was brusque and cavalier in her

treatment of her fellow-students, nothing could exceed the gentle respect with which she instinctively treated women older than herself. She had that inborn sense of the privileges and rights of age which is perhaps the rarest and most lovable attribute of youth.

The ladies remained for half an hour, and they spent three-and-six.

"I think I have seen you sometimes at the Baptist Chapel," said the one with the eyeglass, as they rose to go.

"Yes, I have been there sometimes with my cousin."

"Have you been baptised?" asked the one who had no distinguishing feature.

"Oh yes!" said Mona, rather taken aback by the question.

"I notice you don't stay to the Communion," said the one with the curls.

"I was baptised in the Church of England."

"Oh!" said all three at once, in a tone that made Mona feel herself an utter fraud.

"You must have a talk with Mr Stuart," said the one with the eyeglass, recovering herself first. Every one agreed that she was the "cliverest" of the sisters.

"Yes," said the others, catching eagerly at a method of reconciling Christian charity and fidelity to principle; and, with inquiries after Miss Simpson, they left the shop.

"It would be the Miss Bonthrons," said Rachel, when she heard Mona's description of the new customers. "They are a great deal looked up to in Kirkstoun. Their father was senior deacon in the Baptist Chapel for years, and the pulpit was all draped with black when he died. He has left them very well provided for, too."

Meanwhile Matilda Cookson had found an object in life, and was happy. It was well for her that her enthusiastic devotion to Mona was weighted by the ballast of conscientious work, or her last state might have been worse than her first. As it was, she laboured hard, and when her family inquired the cause of her sudden fit of diligence, she took a pride in looking severely mysterious. Miss Maclean was a princess in disguise, and she was the sole custodian of the great secret. The constant effort to refrain from confiding it, even to her sister, was, in its way, as valuable a bit of moral discipline as was the laborious translation of the *Geier-Wally.*

"I would have come sooner," she said one day to Mona at Castle Maclean, "but my people can't see why I want to walk on the beach at this time of year, and it is so difficult to get rid of Clarinda. Of course if they knew you were Lady Munro's niece they would be only too glad that I should meet you anywhere, but I have not breathed a syllable of that."

She spoke with pardonable pride. She had not yet learned to spare Mona's feelings, and the latter sighed involuntarily.

"Thank you," she said; "but I don't want you to meet me 'on the sly.'"

"I thought of that. Mother would not be at all pleased at my getting to know you as things are, or as she thinks they are; but if there was a row, and she found out that you were Lady Munro's niece, she would more than forgive me. You will tell people who you are some time, won't you?"

For, after all, in what respect is a princess in disguise better than other people, if the story has no *dénouement?*

"I wish very much," said Mona, patiently, "that you would try to see the matter from my point of view. I have taken no pains to pre-

vent people from finding out who my other
relatives are ; but, as a matter of personal taste,
I prefer that they should not talk of it. Besides,
it is just as unpleasant to me to be labelled
Lady Munro's niece, as to be labelled Miss Simpson's cousin. People who really care for me,
care for myself."

Matilda had been straining her eyes in the
direction of "yonder shining light," and she
certainly thought she saw it. The difficulty
was to keep it in view when she was talking to
her mother or Clarinda.

"You know I care for you yourself," she said.
"I don't think I ever cared for anybody so much
in my life."

"Hush-sh ! It is not wise to talk like that
when you know me so little. If the scale turns,
you will hate me all the more because you speak
so strongly now."

"*Hate you !*" laughed Matilda, with the
sublime confidence of eighteen.

"How goes *Geier-Wally* ?"

Mona had a decided gift for teaching, and the
next half-hour passed pleasantly for both of
them. Then, in a very shamefaced way,
Matilda drew a letter from her pocket. "I

wanted to tell you," she said, " I have been writing to—to—my friend."

Her face turned crimson as she spoke. She had met Mona several times, but this was the first reference either of them had made to the original subject of debate.

" Have you ? " said Mona, quietly.

" Yes. Would you mind reading the letter ? I should like to know if there is anything I ought to alter."

Mona read the letter. It was headed by a showy crest and address-stamp, and it was without exception the most pathetic and the most ridiculous production she had ever seen. It was very long, and very sentimental; it made repeated reference to "your passionate love"; and, to Mona's horror, it wound up with the line about the martyrs.

However, it had one saving feature. Between the beginning and the end, Matilda did contrive to give expression to the conviction that she had done wrong in meeting her correspondent, and to the determination that she never would do it again. Compared with this everything else mattered little.

" Is that what you would have said ? "

she asked eagerly, as Mona finished reading it.

"It would be valueless if it were," said Mona, smiling. "He wants your views, not mine. But in quoting that line you are creating for yourself a lofty tradition that will not always be easy to live up to. I speak to myself as much as to you, for it was I who set you the example—for evil or good. You and I burn our boats when we allow ourselves to repeat a line like that."

"I want to burn them," said Matilda, eagerly, only half understanding what was in Mona's mind. "I am quite sure you have burned yours. Then you don't want me to write it over again?"

"No," said Mona, reflectively. "You have said definitely what you intended to say, and few girls could have done as much under the circumstances. Moreover, you have said it in your own way, and that is better than saying it in some one else's way. No, I would not write it over again."

"Thanks, awfully. I am very glad you think it will do. It is a great weight off my mind to have it done. I owe a great deal to you, Miss Maclean."

"I owe you a great deal," said Mona, colouring. "You have taught me a lesson against hasty judgment. When you came into the shop to buy blue ribbon, I certainly did not think you capable of that amount of moral pluck," and she glanced at the letter on Matilda's lap.

"What you must have thought of us!" exclaimed Matilda, blushing in her turn. "Two stuck-up, provincial — cats! Tell me, Miss Maclean, did Dr Dudley know then—what I know about you?"

Matilda was progressing. She saw that Mona winced at the unceasing reference to Lady Munro, so she attempted a periphrasis.

"He does not know now."

"Then I shall like Dr Dudley as long as I live. He is sarcastic and horrid, but he must be one of the people you were talking of the other day who see the invisible."

For Mona had got into the way of giving utterance to her thoughts almost without reserve when Matilda Cookson was with her. It was pleasant to see the look of rapt attention on the girl's face, and Mona did not realise—or realising, she did not care — how little her

companion understood. Mona's talk ought to
have been worth listening to in those days
when her life was so destitute of companionship; but the harvest of her thought was
carried away by the winds and the waves, and
only a few stray gleanings fell into the eager
outstretched hands of Matilda Cookson. Yet
the girl was developing, as plants develop on
a warm damp day in spring, and Mona was
unspeakably grateful to her. The Colonel's
story had not interfered with Mona's determination to "take up each day with both hands,
and live it with all her might;" but it certainly
had not made it any easier to see the ideal in
the actual. Here, however, was one little
human soul who clung to her, depended on her,
learnt from her; and it would have been difficult to determine on which side the balance
of benefit really lay.

CHAPTER XXX.

MR STUART'S TROUBLES.

VERY slowly the days and weeks went by, but at last the end of November drew near. The coast was bleak and cold now, and it was only on exceptionally fine days that Mona could spend a quiet hour at Castle Maclean. When she escaped from the shop she went for a scramble along the coast; and when physical exercise was insufficient to drive away the cobwebs, she walked out to the Colonel's wood to see old Jenny, or, farther still, beyond Kilwinnie to have a chat with Auntie Bell.

With the latter she struck up quite a cordial friendship, and she had the doubtful satisfaction of hearing the Colonel's yarn corroborated in Auntie Bell's quaint language.

"Rachel's queer, ye ken," said Auntie Bell, as

Mona took her farewell in the exquisitely kept, old-fashioned garden. "She's a' for the kirk and the prayer-meetin'; an' yet she's aye that keen tae forgather wi' her betters."

"She wants to make the best of both worlds, I suppose," said Mona. "Poor soul! I am afraid she has not succeeded very well as regards this one."

"Na," said Auntie Bell, tersely. "An' between wersels, I hae ma doots o' the ither."

Mona laughed. It was curious how she and Auntie Bell touched hands across all the oceans that lay between them.

"Are ye muckle ta'en up wi' this 'gran' bazaar,' as they ca' it?"

"Not a bit," said Mona; "I hate bazaars."

"Eh, but we're o' ae mind there!" and Auntie Bell clapped her hands with sufficient emphasis to start an upward rush of crows from the field beyond the hedge.

Nearly half the county at this time was talking of one thing and of only one—the approaching bazaar at Kirkstoun. It was almost incredible to Mona that so trifling an event should cause so much excitement; but bazaars, like earthquakes, vary in importance according to the part of the world in which they occur.

And this was no sale for church or chapel, at which the men could pretend to sneer, and which a good burgher might consistently refuse to attend; it was essentially the bazaar of the stronger sex—except in so far as the weaker sex did all the work in connection with it; it was for no less an object than the new town hall.

For many years the inhabitants of Kirkstoun had felt that their town hall was a petty, insignificant building, out of all proportion to the size and importance of the burgh; and after much deliberation they had decided on the bold step of erecting a new building, and of looking mainly to Providence—spelt with a capital, of course—for the funds.

All this, however, was now rapidly becoming a matter of ancient history; the edifice had been complete for some time; about one-third of the expense had been defrayed; and, in order that the debt might be cleared off with a clean sweep, the ladies of the town had " kindly consented " to hold a bazaar.

" Man's extremity is woman's opportunity " had been the graceful, if not original, remark of one of the local bailies; but men are proverbially ungrateful, and this view of the matter had not been the only one mooted.

" Kindly consented, indeed ! " one carping spirit had growled. " Pretty consent any of you would have given if it had not been an opportunity for dressing yourselves up and having a ploy. Whose pockets is all the money to come out of first or last ? That's what I would like to know ! "

It is quite needless to remark that the first of these speeches had been made on the platform, the second in domestic privacy.

Like wildfire the enthusiasm had spread. All through the summer, needles had flown in and out; paint-brushes had been flourished somewhat wildly; cupboards had been ransacked; begging-letters had been written to friends all over the country, and to every man who, in the memory of the inhabitants, had left Kirkstoun to make his fortune " abroad."

It was very characteristic of " Kirkstoun folk " that not many of these letters had been written in vain. Kirkstoun men are clannish. Scatter as they may over the whole known world, they stand together shoulder to shoulder like a well-trained regiment.

The bazaar was to be held for three days before Christmas, and was to be followed by a grand ball. Was not this excitement enough to fill the imagination of every girl for many miles around? The matrons had a harder time of it, as they usually have, poor souls! With them lay the solid responsibility of getting together a sufficiency of work—and alas for all the jealousies and heart-burnings this involved!—with them lay the planning of ball-dresses that were to cost less, and look better, than any one else's; with them lay the necessity of coaxing and conciliating "your papa."

Rachel Simpson was not a person of sufficient social importance to be a stall-holder, or a receiver of goods; and she certainly was not one of those women who are content to work that others may shine, so Mona had taken little or no interest in the projected bazaar.

One morning, however, she received a letter from Doris which roused her not a little.

"Kirkstoun is somewhere near Borrowness, is it not?" wrote her friend. "If so, I shall see you before Christmas. Those friends of mine at St Rules, to whom you declined an introduction, have a stall at the Town Hall bazaar, and I am going over to assist them. It is a kind of debt, for they helped me with my last enterprise of the kind, but I should contrive to get out of it except for the prospect of seeing you.

"You will come to the bazaar, of course : I should think you would be ready for a little dissipation by that time ; and I will promise to be merciful if you will visit my stall."

"How delightful !" was Mona's first thought ; "how disgusting !" was her second ; "how utterly out of keeping Doris will be with me and my surroundings !" was her conclusion. "Ponies and pepper-pots do not harmonise very well with shops and poor relations. But, fortunately, the situation is not of my making."

She was still meditating over the letter when Rachel came in looking flushed and excited.

"Mona," she said, "I have made a nice little engagement for you. You know you say you like singing ? "

"Yes," said Mona, with an awful premonition of what might be coming.

"I met Mr Stuart on the Kirkstoun road just now. He was that put about! . Two of his best speakers for the *soirée* to-night have fallen through, he says. Mr Roberts has got the jaundice, and Mr Dowie has had to go to the funeral of a friend. Mr Stuart said the whole thing would be a failure, and he was fairly at his wits' end. You see there's no time to do anything now. He said if he could get a song or a recitation, or anything, it would do; so of course I told him you were a fine singer, and I was sure you would give us a song. You should have seen how his face brightened up. 'Capital!' said he; 'I have noticed her singing in church. Perhaps she would give us "I know that my Redeemer liveth," or something of that kind?'"

"My dear cousin," said Mona, at last finding breath to speak, "you might just as well ask me to give a performance on the trapeze. I have never *sung* since I was in Germany. It is one thing to chirp to you in the firelight, and quite another to stand up on a public platform and perform. The thing is utterly absurd."

"Hoots," said Rachel, "they are not so particular. Many's the time I have seen them pleased with worse singing than yours."

Then ensued the first 'stand-up fight' between the two.   As her cousin waxed hotter
Mona waxed cooler, and finally she ended the
discussion by setting out to speak to Mr Stuart
herself.

She found him in his comfortable study, his
slippered feet on the fender, and a polemico-
religious novel in his hand.

"I am sorry to find my cousin has made
an engagement for me this evening," she said.
"It is quite impossible for me to fulfil it."

"Oh, nonsense!" he said, kindly.   "It is
too late to withdraw now.   Your name is in
the programme," and he glanced at the neatly
written paper on his writing-table, as if it had
been a legal document at the least.   "My wife
is making copies of that for all the speakers.
You can't draw back now."

"It might be too late to withdraw," said
Mona, "if I had ever put myself forward; but,
although my cousin meant to act kindly to
every one concerned, she and I are two distinct
people."

"Come, come! Of course I quite understand your feeling a little shy, if you are not
used to singing in public; but you will be all

right as soon as you begin. I remember my
first sermon — what a state I was in, to be
sure! And yet they told me it was a great
success."

"I am very sorry," said Mona. "It is not
mere nervousness and shyness—though there is
that too, of course—it is simply that I am not
qualified to do it."

"We are not very critical. There won't be
more than three persons present who know good
singing from bad."

"Unfortunately I should wish to sing for
those three."

"Ah," he said, with a curl of his lip, "you
must have appreciation. The lesson some of
us have got to learn in life, Miss Maclean, is
to do without appreciation." He paused, but
her look of sudden interest was inviting. "One
is tempted sometimes to think that one could
speak to so much more purpose in a world
where there is some intellectual life, where
people are not wholly blind to the problems
of the day; but to preach Sunday after Sunday
to those who have no eyes to see, no ears to
hear, to suppress one's best thoughts——"

He stopped short.

" It is a pity surely to do that, unless one is a prophet indeed."

" Ah," he said, " you cannot understand my position. It is a singular one, unique perhaps. —You will sing for us to-night ? "

" Mr Stuart," said Mona, struggling against the temptation to speak sharply, " I should not have left my work to come here in the busiest time of the day, if I had been prepared to yield in the end. And indeed why should I ? There are plenty of people in the neighbourhood who sing as well as I ; and people who are well known have a right to claim a little indulgence. I have none. It is not even as if I were a member of the Chapel."

" I hope you will be soon."

" Well," said Mona, rising with a smile, " you have more pressing claims on your attention at present than my conversion to Baptist principles. Good morning."

" Yes," he said, reproachfully, " I must go out in this rain, and try to beat up a substitute for you. A country minister's life is no sinecure, Miss Maclean ; and his work is doubled when he feels the necessity of keeping pace

with the times." He glanced at the book he
had laid down.

"I suppose so," said Mona, somewhat hypocritically. She longed to make a very different
reply, but she was glad to escape on any terms.
"I wish you all success in your search. You
will not go far before you find a fitter makeshift
than I."

"I doubt it," he said, going with her to the
door. "Did any young lady's education ever
yet fit her to do a thing frankly and gracefully,
when she was asked to do it ?"

Mona sighed. "Education is a long word,
Mr Stuart," she said. "It savours more of
eternity than of time. 'So many worlds, so
much to do.' If we should meet in another life,
perhaps I shall be able to sing for you then."

He was absolutely taken aback. What did
she mean ? Was she really poaching in his
preserves ? It was his privilege surely to give
the conversation a religious turn, and he did
not see exactly how she had contrived to do
it. However, it was his duty to rise to the
occasion, even although the effort might involve
a severe mental dislocation.

"I hope we shall sing together there," he said, "with crowns on our heads, and palms in our hands."

It was Mona's turn to be taken aback. She had not realised the effect of her unconventional remarks, when tried by a conventional standard.

"*Behüte Gott!*" she said as she made her way home in the driving rain. "There are worse fates conceivable than annihilation."

Rachel was severely dignified all day, but she was anxious that Mona should go with her to the *soirée*, so she was constrained to bury the hatchet before evening. Mona was much relieved when things had slipped back into their wonted course. Her life was a fiasco indeed if she failed to please Rachel Simpson.

CHAPTER XXXI.

STRADIVARIUS.

THE chapel doors were open, and a bright light streamed across the gravelled enclosure on to the dreary street beyond. People were flocking in, talking and laughing, in eager anticipation of pleasures to come; and a number of hungry-eyed children clung to the railing, and gazed at the promise of good things within.

And indeed the promise was a very palpable one. Mona had scarcely entered the outer door when she was presented with a large earthenware cup and saucer, a pewter spoon, and a well-filled baker's bag.

"What am I to do with these?" she asked, aghast.

"Take them in with you, of course," said Rachel. "You can look inside the bag, but you mustn't eat anything till the interval."

Mona thought she could so far control her curiosity as to await the appointed time, but her strength of mind was not subjected to this test. A considerable proportion of the assembled congregation were children, and most of them were engaged in laying out cakes, sweet biscuits, apples, pears, figs, almonds, and raisins, in a tempting row on the book-board, somewhat to the detriment of the subjacent hymn-books.

"They ordered three hundred bags at three-pence each," said Rachel, in a loud whisper. "It's wonderful how much you get for the money; and they say Mr Philp makes a pretty profit out of it too. I suppose it's the number makes it pay. The cake's plain, to be sure; I always think it would be better if it were richer, and less of it. But there's the children to think of, of course."

At this moment a loud report echoed through the church. Mona started, and had vague thoughts of gunpowder plots, but the explosion was only the work of an adventurous boy, who had tied up his sweets in a handkerchief of doubtful antecedents, that he might have the satisfaction of blowing up and bursting his bag. This feat was pretty frequently repeated in the

course of the evening, in spite of all the moral
and physical influence brought to bear on the
offenders by Mr Stuart and the parents re-
spectively.

The chapel was intensely warm when the
speakers took their places on the platform, and
Mona fervently hoped that Mr Stuart had failed
to find a stopgap, as the programme was already
of portentous length. It seemed impossible that
she could sit out the evening in such an atmosphere, and still more impossible that the blood-
less, neurotic girl in front of her should do so.

The first speaker was introduced by the chair-
man.

"Now for the moral windbags!" thought
Mona, resignedly.

She felt herself decidedly snubbed, however,
when the speeches were in full swing. The gift
of speaking successfully at a *soirée* is soon
recognised in the world where *soirées* prevail,
and the man who possesses it acquires a celeb-
rity often extending beyond his own county.
One or two of the speakers were men possessing
both wit and humour, of a good Scotch brand;
and the others made up for their deficiencies in
this respect by a clever and laborious patch-

work of anecdotes and repartees, which, in the excitement of the moment, could scarcely be distinguished from the genuine mantle of happy inspiration.

In the midst of one of the speeches a disturbance arose. The girl in front of Mona had fainted. Several men carried her out, shyly and clumsily, in the midst of a great commotion ; and, after a moment's hesitation, Mona followed them. She was glad she had done so, for fainting-fits were rare on that breezy coast, and no one else seemed to know what to do. Meanwhile the unfortunate girl was being held upright in the midst of a small crowd of spectators.

"Lay her down on the matting," said Mona, quietly, "and stand back, please, all of you. No, she wants nothing under her head. One of you might fetch some water — and a little whisky, if it is at hand. It is nothing serious. Mrs Brander and I can do all that is required."

All the men started off for water at once, much to Mona's relief. She loosened the girl's dress, while the matron produced smelling-salts, and in a few minutes the patient opened her eyes, with a deep sigh.

"Surely Kirkstoun is not her home," said Mona, looking at the girl's face. "Sea-breezes have not had much to do with the making of her."

"Na," said the matron. "She's a puir weed. She's visiting her gran'faither across the street. I'll tak' her hame."

"No, no," said Mona. "Go back to the *soirée*, I'll look after her."

"Ye'll miss your tea! They're takin' roun' the teapits the noo."

"I have had tea, thank you," and, putting a strong arm round the girl's waist, Mona walked home with her, and saw her safely into bed.

She hurried back to the chapel, for she knew Rachel would be fretting about her; but the night breeze was cold and fresh, and she dreaded returning to that heated, impure air. When she entered the door, however, she scarcely noticed the atmosphere, for the laughing and fidgeting had given place to an intense stillness, broken only by one rich musical voice.

> "So my eye and hand,
> And inward sense that works along with both,
> Have hunger that can never feed on coin."

Mr Stuart's stopgap was filling his part of the programme.

Mona hesitated at the door, and then quietly resumed her place at the end of the pew beside Rachel. The reader paused for a moment till she was seated, a scarcely perceptible shade of expression passed over his face, as her silk gown rustled softly up the aisle, and then he went on.

It was a curious poem to read to such an audience, but even the boys and girls forgot their almonds and raisins as they listened to the beautiful voice. For Mona, the low ceiling, the moist walls, and the general air of smug squalor vanished like a dissolving view. In their place the infinite blue of an Italian sky rose above her head, the soft warm breeze of the south was on her cheek; and she stood in the narrow picturesque street listening to the " plain white - aproned man," with the light of the eternal in his eyes.

> " 'Tis God gives skill,
> But not without men's hands : He could not make
> Antonio Stradivari's violins
> Without Antonio.   Get thee to thy easel."

It was over.   There was a long breath, and a general movement in the chapel.   Dudley took an obscure seat at the back of the platform, shaded his eyes with his hand, and looked at Mona.

Again and again in London he had told himself that it was all illusion, that he had exaggerated the nobility of her face, the sensitiveness of her mouth, the subtle air of distinction about her whole appearance; and now he knew that he had exaggerated nothing. His eye wandered round the congregation, and came back to her with a sensation of infinite rest. Then his pulse began to beat more quickly. He was excited, perhaps, by the way in which that uncultured audience had sat spellbound by his voice, for at that moment it seemed to him that he would give a great deal to call up the love-light in those eloquent eyes.

"She is a girl," he thought, with quick intuition. "She has never loved, and no doubt she believes she never will. I envy the man who forces her to own her mistake. She is no sweet white daisy to whom any man's touch is sunshine. There are depths of expression in that face that have never yet been stirred. Happy man who is the first—perhaps the only one—to see them! He will have a long account to settle with Fortune."

And then Dudley pulled himself up short. Thoughts like these would not lead to success in his examination. And even if they would, what right had he to think them? Till his Intermediate was over in July, he must speak to no woman of love; and not until his Final lay behind him had he any right to think of marriage. And any day while he was far away in London the man might come—the man with the golden key——

Dudley turned and bowed to the speaker in considerable confusion. Some graceful reference had evidently been made to his reading, for there was a momentary pause in the vague droning that had accompanied his day-dreams, and every one was looking at him with a cordial smile.

"Who would have thought of Dr Dudley being here?" said Rachel, as the cousins walked home. "It is a great pity his being so short-sighted; he looks so much nicer without his spectacles. I wonder if he remembers what good friends we were that day at St Rules?—I declare I believe that's him behind us now."

She was right, and he was accompanied by no less a person than the Baptist minister.

"I would ask you to walk out and have a bachelor's supper with me, Stuart, by way of getting a little pure air into your lungs," Dudley had said, as he threw on his heavy Inverness cape; "but it is a far cry, and I suppose you have a guest at your house to-night."

The minister had accepted with alacrity. He was tired, to be sure, but he would gladly have walked ten miles for the sake of a conversation with one of his "intellectual peers."

"I have no guest," he had said, eagerly; "it was my man who failed me. I would ask you to come home with me, but there are things we cannot talk of before my wife. 'Leave thou thy sister,'—you know."

A faint smile had flitted over Dudley's face at the thought of Mr Stuart's "purer air."

So they set out, and in due course they overtook Rachel and Mona.

Mr Stuart could scarcely believe his eyes when he saw Dr Dudley actually slackening his pace to walk with them. It was right and Christian to be courteous, no doubt, but this was so utterly uncalled for.

Dudley did not seem to think so, however. He exchanged a few pleasant words with Rachel, and then, regardless alike of her delight and of the minister's irritation, he very simply and naturally walked on with Mona in advance of the other two.

Many a time, when hundreds of miles had separated them, Mona and Dudley had in imagination talked to each other frankly and simply; but, now that they were together, they both became suddenly shy and timid. What were their mutual relations? Were they old friends, or mere acquaintances? Neither knew.

The silence became awkward.

"Your reading was a great treat," said Mona, somewhat formally at last.

Anybody could have told him that. He wanted something more from her.

"I am glad if it did not bore you," he said, coldly.

She looked up. They were just leaving the last of the Kirkstoun street-lamps behind them, but in the uncertain light they exchanged a smile. That did more for them than many words.

"It is not poetry of course," he said. "It is only a magnificent instance of what my shaggy old Edinburgh professor would call 'metrical intellection.'"

"And yet, surely, in a broader sense, it is poetry. It seems to me that that magnificent 'genius of morality' produces art of a kind peculiarly its own. It is not cleverness; it is inspiration—though it is not 'poesie.' In any case, you made it poetry for me. I *saw* the sunny, glowing street, and the blue sky overhead."

"Did you?" he said, eagerly. "Truly? I am so glad. I had such a vivid mental picture of it myself, that I thought the brain-waves must carry it to some one. It is very dark here. Won't you take my arm?"

"No, thank you; I am well used to this road in the dark. By the way, I must apologise for disturbing your reading. I would have remained at the door, but I was afraid some man would offer me his seat, and that we should between us kick the foot-board and knock down a few hymn - books before we settled the matter."

"I was so relieved when you came forward and took your own place," he said slowly, as though he were determined that she should not take the words for an idle compliment. "I had been watching that vacant corner beside Miss Simpson. How is Castle Maclean?"

"It is pretty well delivered over to the sea-gulls at present. I am afraid it must be admitted that Castle Maclean is more suited to a summer than to a winter residence. I often run down there, but these east winds are not suggestive of lounging."

"Not much," he said. "When I picture you there, it is always summer."

"Oh," said Mona, suddenly, "there is one thing that I must tell you. You remember a conversation we had about the Cooksons?"

"Yes."

"Matilda and I are great friends now, and I have had good reason to be ashamed of my original attitude towards her. I think it was you who put me right."

"Indeed it was not," he said, warmly. "I, forsooth! You put yourself right—if you were ever wrong."

"I was wrong. And you—well, you took too high an estimate of me, and that is the surest way of putting people right. You have no idea how much good stuff there is in that child. She is becoming quite a German scholar; and she has read *Sesame and Lilies*, has been much struck by that quotation from Coventry

Patmore, and at the present moment is deep in
Heroes. What do you say to that?"

"Score!" he said, quietly. "How did she
come to know you?"

"Oh, by one of the strange little accidents of
life. She has done me a lot of good, too. She
is very warm-hearted and impressionable."

There was a lull in the conversation. Across
the bare fields came the distant roar of the sea.
They were still nearly half a mile from home,
and a great longing came upon Mona to tell
him about her medical studies. Why had she
been such an idiot as to make that promise;
and, having made it, why had she never asked
her cousin to release her from it? She drew a
long breath.

"My dear," said Rachel's voice behind them,
"Mr Stuart wants to have a little conversation
with you. Well, doctor, I hope Mrs Hamilton
is not worse, that you are here just now?"

Mr Stuart's wrongs were avenged.

For one moment Dudley thought of protest-
ing, but the exchange of partners was already
effected, and he was forced to submit.

"Our conversation was left unfinished this
morning, Miss Maclean," said the minister.

"Was it? I thought we had discussed the subject in all its bearings. You are to be congratulated on the substitute you found."

"Am I not?" he answered, warmly. "It was all by accident, too, that I met the doctor, and he was very unwilling to come. He had just run down for one day to settle a little business matter for his aunt; but I put him near the end of the programme, so that he might not have to leave the house till near Mrs Hamilton's bedtime."

For one day! For one day!

The minister sighed. Miss Simpson had left him no choice about "speaking to" her cousin; but he did not feel equal to an encounter tonight; and certainly he could scarcely have found Mona in a less approachable mood.

"You are not a Baptist, Miss Maclean?"

"No."

"Have you studied the subject at all?"

"The Gospels are not altogether unfamiliar ground to me," but her tone was much less aggressive than her words.

"And to what conclusion do they bring you?"

"I think there is a great deal to be said in

favour of the Baptist view ; but, Mr Stuart, it all seems to me a matter of so little importance. Surely it is the existence, not the profession, of faith that redeems the world ; and the precise mode of profession is of less importance still."

" Do you realise what you are saying ? " Mr Stuart began to forget his fatigue. " God has declared that one 'mode of profession,' as you call it, is in accordance with His will, but you pay no heed, because your finite reason tells you that it is of so little importance."

" It is God who is responsible for my finite reason, not I," said Mona ; and then the thought of where this conversation must lead, and the uselessness of it, overwhelmed her.

Her voice softened. " Mr Stuart," she said, " it is very kind of you to care what I think and believe—to-night, too, of all times, when you must be so tired after that 'function.' I believe it is a help to some people to talk, but I don't think it is even right for me—at least at present. When I begin to formulate things, I seem to lose the substance in the shadow ; I get interested in the argument for the argument's sake. Believe me, I am not living a thoughtless life."

Mr Stuart was impressed by her earnestness in spite of himself. "But, my dear young lady, is it wise, is it safe, to leave things so vague, to have nothing definite to lean upon?"

"I think so; if one tries to do right."

"It is all very well while you are young, and life seems long; but trouble will come, and sickness, and death——"

Rachel and Dudley had reached the gate of Carlton Lodge, and were waiting for the other two. But Mr Stuart did not think it necessary to break off, or even to lower his voice.

"——and when the hour of your need comes, and you can no longer grapple with great thoughts, will you not long for a definite word, a text——?"

Dudley's face was a picture. Mona underwent a quick revulsion of feeling. How dared any one speak to her publicly like that! She answered lightly, however, too lightly—

> "'Denn, was man schwarz auf weiss besitzt,
> Kann man getrost nach Hause tragen'"!

Of course she knew that Dr Dudley alone would understand, and of course Dudley keenly appreciated the apt quotation.

" Holloa, Stuart ! " he said, " you seem to be
figuring in a new and alarming *rôle*. I am
half afraid to go in with you. I wish you
could come and join in our discussion, Miss
Maclean. 'Nineteenth Century Heretics' is
our topic. Stuart takes the liberal side, I the
conservative."

"Do you think it expedient," said the
minister reproachfully, as the two men crunched
the gravel of the carriage-drive beneath their
feet, " to talk in that flippant way to women on
deep subjects ? "

"Oh, Miss Maclean is all right ! She could
knock you and me into a cocked-hat any
day."

And he believed what he said—at least so far
as the minister was concerned.

" She really is very intelligent," admitted Mr
Stuart. " I quite miss her face when she is not
at church on Sunday morning; but you know
she does put herself forward a little. What
made her go out after that fainting girl, when
so many older women were present ? Oh, I
forgot, you had not arrived——"

"It was well for the fainting girl that she
did," interrupted Dudley, calmly. " When I was

going to the vestry some one rushed frantically against me, and told me a woman had fainted. I arrived on the scene a moment after Miss Maclean, but fortunately she did not see me. By Jingo, Stuart, that girl can rise to an occasion! If ever your chapel is crowded, and takes fire, you may pray that Miss Maclean may be one of the congregation."

It gave him a curious pleasure to talk like this, but he would not have trusted himself to say so much, had it not been for the friendly darkness, and the noise of the gravel beneath their feet.

Mr Stuart suspected nothing. Dr Dudley and Rachel Simpson's cousin! People would have been very slow to link their names.

"Yes, she is very intelligent," he repeated. "I must try to find time to have some more talks with her."

"I wish you joy of them!" thought Dudley. "I should like to know how you tackle a case like that, Stuart," he said. "Tell me what you said to her, and what she said to you."

CHAPTER XXXII.

CHUMS.

ACTION and reaction are equal and opposite.

Dudley was back in his den in London. For the first day after his return, he had thought of nothing but Mona; her face had come between him and everything he did. Now it was bending, grave and motherly, over the fainting girl, now it was sparkling with mischief at the quotation from *Faust*, now it vibrated to the words of *Stradivarius*, and now—oftenest of all—it looked up at him in the dim lamplight, with that inquiring, inexplicable smile, half friendly, half defiant.

And the evening and the morning were the first day.

But now the second day had come, and Dudley was thinking—of Rachel Simpson.

He pushed aside his books, and tramped up and down the room. How came she there, his exquisite fern, in that hideous dungeon? And was she indeed so fair? Removed from those surroundings, would she begin for the first time to show the taint she had acquired? In the drawing-room, at the dinner-table, in a *solitude à deux*, what if one should see in her a suggestion of—Rachel Simpson?

And then Mona's face came back once more, pure, high-souled, virgin; without desire or thought for love and marriage. There was not the faintest ruby streak on the bud, and yet, and yet—what if he were the man to call it forth? Why had she refused his arm? It would have been pleasant to feel the touch of that strong, self-reliant little hand. It would be pleasant to feel it now——

There was a knock at the door, and a fair-haired, merry-eyed young man came in.

"Holloa, Melville!" said Dudley. "Off duty?"

"Ay; Johnston and I have swopped nights this week."

"Anything special on at the hospital?"

"No, nothing since I saw you. That Viking is not going to pull through, after all."

" You don't mean it ! "

" Fact. I believe that bed is unlucky. This is the third case that has died in it. All pneumonia, too."

" I believe pneumonia cases ought to be isolated."

" I know you have a strong theory to that effect. I did an external strabismus to-day."

" Successful ? "

" I think so. I kept my hair on. By the way, you remember that duffer Lawson ? "

" Yes."

" He has hooked an heiress—older than himself, but not so bad-looking. He will have a practice in no time now. I met him bowling along in his carriage, and there was I trudging through the mud ! It's the irony of fate, upon my soul ! "

" True," said Dudley ; " but you know, when we have all the intellect, and all the heart, and all the culture, we don't need to grudge him his carriage."

" I'll shy something at you, Ralph ! And now I want your news. How is the way ? "

" Thorny."

" And the prospect of the anatomy medal ? "

"Dim.   But what are medals to an 'aged, aged man' like me?"

"You are hipped to-night.   What's up?"

Dudley did not reply at once.   He was intensely reserved, as a rule, about his private affairs, but a curious impulse was upon him now to contradict his own character.

"You and I have been chums for twenty years, more or less, Jack," he said, irrelevantly.

"True, O king!   Well?"

"I want to ask your advice on an abstract case."

"Do you?   Fire away!   I am a dab at medical etiquette."   Dudley had been paying a few professional visits for a friend.

"It is not a question of medical etiquette," he said, testily.   "Suppose," he drew a long breath—"suppose you knew a young girl——"

"Ah!   My dear fellow, I never do know a young girl!   It is the greatest mistake in the world."

"Suppose," went on Dudley, unheeding, "that physically, mentally, and morally, she was about as near perfection as a human being can be."

"Oh, *of course!*"

"I don't ask your opinion as to the probability of it. I don't say I know such a person. Man alive! can't you suppose an abstract case?"

"It is a large order, but I am doing my level best."

"Suppose that, so far as she was concerned, it was simply all over with you."

"Oh, that is easy enough. Well?"

"Would you marry her, if——"

"Alack, it had to come! Yes. If——?"

"If she was a—a tremendous contrast to her people?"

"Oh, *that* is it, is it?" Melville sprang to his feet, and spoke very emphatically. "No, my dear fellow, upon my soul, I would not! They grow into their heredity with all the certainty of fate. I would rather marry a *gauche* and unattractive girl because her mother was charming."

This was rather beside the point, but it depressed Dudley, and he sighed.

"But suppose — one has either to rave or make use of conventional expressions—suppose she was infinitely bright, and attractive, and womanly?"

"Oh, they are all that, you know."

" If you knew her——"

" Oh, of course. That goes without saying. Now we come back to the point we started from. As I told you before, I never do know them, and it keeps me out of a world of mischief."

Melville seated himself by the fire, and buried his hands in his curly hair.

" Ralph, while we are at it," he said, " I want to give you a word of advice. *Verb. sap.*, you know. If any man knows you, I am that man. As you were remarking, you have lain on my dissecting-board for twenty years."

" I wish you had done me under water. You would have made a neater thing of it."

" So I would, old fellow, but you were too big. The difficulty was to get you into my mental laboratory at all."

Dudley bowed.

" Don't bow. It was well earned. You fished for it uncommon neatly. But you know, Ralph, I am serious now. Let me say it for once — you are awfully fastidious, awfully sensitive, awfully over-cultured. Few women could please you. It matters little

whether you marry a good woman or a bad,
—I don't know that there is much difference
between them myself; the saints and the
sinners get jumbled somehow,—but you must
marry a woman of the world. Gretchen would
be awfully irresistible, I know—for a month;
she would not wear. Marry a woman full of
surprises, a woman who does not take all her
colour from you, a woman who can keep you
dangling, as it were."

"It sounds restful."

Melville laughed. "Restful or not, that's
the woman for you, Ralph. You are not equal
to an hour at the Pavilion, I suppose? Well,
ta-ta."

Dudley sat in silence till the echo of his
friend's steps on the pavement had died away.
Then he rose and tramped up and down the
room again.

"After all, Miss Simpson is only her cousin,"
he said. "If I routed about I might find some
rather shady cousins myself. But then I don't
live with them. If her parents were a decided
cut above that, how comes she there? And
being there, how can she have escaped con-
tamination? I wonder what Miss Simpson's

dinner-table is like ? Ugh ! Is it as squalid as the shop ? And why is the shop so squalid ? Does Miss Simpson allow no interference in her domain ? And yet I cannot conceive of Miss Maclean being out of place at a duchess's table."

He dropped into a chair, clasped his hands behind his head, and spoke aloud almost indignantly in his perplexity.

"How can a provincial shop-girl be a woman of the world ? And yet, upon my soul ! Miss Maclean seems to me to come nearer Melville's description than any woman I ever knew. Alack-a-day ! I must be besotted indeed. Oh, damn that examination !"

Ralph returned to his books, however, and tried hard to shut out all farther thoughts of Mona that night.

CHAPTER XXXIII.

CARBOLIC!

"Holloa, Jones! going home?"

"I am going to lunch; I may be back in the afternoon."

"Please yourself, my dear fellow, but if you don't finish that axilla to-day, I shall be under the painful necessity of reflecting the pectorals, and proceeding with the thorax, at 9 A.M. to-morrow."

"Oh, I say, Dudley, that is too bad."

"I fail to see it. You have had one day too long as it is."

"But you know I did cut my finger."

"H'm. I have not just the profoundest faith in that cut finger. You know it *did* happen on the day of the football-match."

The boy laughed. "And Collett will never

manage that sole of the foot without you," he
said.

"Collett must." Dudley smiled up at the
eager face that was bending over his dissection.
"I only undertook to find the cutaneous branch
of the internal plantar," and he lifted the nerve
affectionately on the handle of his scalpel.
"Come, Jones, fire away. *Ce n'est pas la mer
à boire.* Half an hour will do it."

"Oh, I say! It would take me four hours.
You know, Dudley, there is such a lot of
reading on the axilla. I am all in a muddle
as it is. I'll sit up half the night reading it,
if you will give me another day."

"Very sorry, old man. *Ars longa.* I must
get on with my thorax. It will do you far
more good to read in the dissecting - room.
Preconceived ideas are a mistake. Get a good
lunch, and come back. That's your scalpel, I
think, Collett."

"Oh, bother! I only wish I had ideas of
any kind! I wish to goodness somebody
would demonstrate the whole thing to me,
and finish the dissection as he goes along!"

"I will do that with pleasure, if you like,
to - morrow. The gain will be mine — and

perhaps it will be the best thing you can do
now. But don't play that little game too often,
if you mean to be an anatomist."

"I don't," cried the boy, vehemently. "I
wish to heaven I need never see this filthy old
hole again!"

Dudley glanced round the fine airy room,
as he stood with his hands under the tap.

"I know that feeling well," he said.

"You, Dudley! Why, somebody said the
other day that the very dust of the dissecting-
room was dear to you."

"So it is, I think," said Ralph, smiling.
"But it was very different in the days when
I stroked the nettle in the gingerly fashion you
are doing now."

"You mean that you think I should like it
better if I really tucked into it," said the boy,
ruefully.

"I don't think at all; I know. 9 A.M. to-
morrow sharp, then."

Dudley stepped out briskly into the raw damp
air. The mud was thick under foot, and the
whole aspect of the world was depressing to the
hard-worked student. One by one the familiar
furrows took possession of his brow, and his step

slackened gradually, till it kept pace with the
dead march of his thoughts. He was within a
stone's-throw of his rooms, when a dashing mail-
phaeton came up behind him. A good horse
was always a source of pleasure to him, and he
noted, point by point, the beauties of the two
fine bays, which, bespattered with foam, were
chafing angrily at the delay caused by some
block in the street. Suddenly Ralph bethought
himself of Melville's story about the "irony of
fate"; and he glanced with amused curiosity at
the occupant of the carriage.

There was no irony here. The reins lay firmly
but easily in the hands of a man who was well
in keeping with the horses,—fine-looking, of
military bearing, with ruddy face, and curly
white hair. He, too, seemed annoyed at the
block, for there was a heavy frown on his
brow.

At last the offending cart turned down a side-
street, and the bays dashed on. Immediately
in front of them was a swift heavy dray, and
behind it, as is the fashion among *gamins*, sublimely regardless of all the dangers of his position, hung a very small boy. The dray stopped
for a moment, then suddenly lumbered on, and

before either Dudley or the driver of the phaeton
had noticed the child, he had fallen from his pre-
carious perch, and lay under the hoofs of the bays.

With one tremendous pull the phaeton was
brought to a standstill, while Dudley and the
groom rushed forward to extricate the child.

"I think he is more frightened than hurt,"
said Ralph, "but my rooms are close at hand.
If you like, I will take him in and examine him
carefully. I am a doctor."

"Upon my soul, I am very much obliged to
you! I am leaving town for the Riviera to-night,
and it would be confoundedly awkward to be
detained by a business of this kind. Step up,
will you? Charles will hand up the child after
you are in."

The boy lay half stunned, drawing little sob-
bing breaths. When they reached the house,
Dudley handed the latch-key to his companion,
and, raising the boy in his strong arms, he carried
him up the steps.

"Bless me, you are as good as a woman!"
said the man of the world, in amused admiration, as he opened the door. "It was uncommonly lucky for me that you happened to be
passing."

Dudley showed his new acquaintance into his snuggery, while he examined the boy. The snuggery was a room worth seeing. There was nothing showy or striking about it, but every picture, every book, every bit of pottery, had been lovingly and carefully chosen, and the *tout ensemble* spoke well for the owner of the room.

" A man of culture clearly," said the visitor, after making a leisurely survey; "and what a life for him, by Gad!—examining dirty little *gamins!* He can't be poor. What the deuce does he do it for?"

" He is all right," said Dudley emphatically, re-entering the room. " He has been much interested in my manikin, and at the present moment is tucking vigorously into bread-and-marmalade. I have assured him that ninety-nine drivers out of a hundred would have gone right over him. You certainly are to be congratulated on the way you pulled those horses up."

"Do you think so? I am very glad to hear it. Gad! I thought myself it was all over with the little chap. The fact is—it is a fine state of affairs if I can't manage a horse at my time of life; but I confess my thoughts were pretty far afield at the moment. It is most annoying. I have taken my berth on the Club Train for this afternoon, and I find I shall have to go without seeing my niece. I wrote to make an appointment, but it seems she has left her former rooms. By the way, you are a doctor. Do you happen to know any of the lady medical students?"

Dudley shook his head. "I am sorry I have not that honour," he said.

His visitor laughed harshly.

"You don't believe in all that, eh?"

"Oh, I don't say that. I am very far from being conservative on the subject of women's work. I am inclined on the whole to think that women have souls, and, that being so, and the age of brute force being past, it is to my mind a natural corollary that they should choose their own work."

"I don't see that at all, sir. I don't see that at all," said the elderly gentleman, throwing himself into a chair, and talking very warmly. "Souls! What have souls got to do with it, I should like to know? Can they do it without becoming blunted? That is the question."

"I confess I think it is a strange life for a woman to choose, but I know one or two women

—one certainly—who would make far better doctors than I ever shall."

"Oh, they are a necessity! Mind, sir, I believe women-doctors are a necessity; so it is a mercy they want to do it; but why the devil should my niece take it up? She is not the sort of woman you mean at all. To think that a fine-looking, gentle, gifted girl, who might marry any man she liked, and move in any society she chose, should spend her days in an atmosphere of—what *is* the smell in this room, sir?"

Dudley laughed. "Carbolic, I suppose," he said. "I use a good deal of it."

"Carbolic! Well, think of a beautiful woman finding it necessary to live in an atmosphere of —*carbolic!*"

Dudley laughed again, his visitor's voice was so expressive.

"There are minor drawbacks, of course," he said. "But I strongly agree with you, that there is a part of our work which ought to be in the hands of women; and I, for one, will gladly hand it over to them."

"I believe you! Oh, when all is said, it's grimy work, doctoring—grimy work!"

"You know, of course, that I join issue with you there."

"You don't find it so?"

"God forbid!"

"Tell me," said the stranger eagerly, running his eye from Dudley's cultured face to his long, nervous hands, "you ought to know—given a woman, pure, and good, and strong, could she go through it all unharmed?"

"Pure, and good, and strong," repeated Dudley, reflectively. "Given a woman like that, you may safely send her through hell itself. I think the fundamental mistake of our civilisation has been educating women as if they were all run in one mould. She will get her eyes opened, of course, if she studies Medicine, but some women never attain the possibilities of their nature in the shadow of convent walls. Frankly, I have no great fancy for artificially reared purity."

"Artificially reared!" exclaimed the other. "My dear sir, there are a few intermediate stages between the hothouse and the dunghill! If it were only art, or literature, or politics, or even science, but anatomy—the dissecting-room!"

"Well," said Dudley rather indignantly, his views developing as he spoke, " even anatomy, like most things, is as you make it. Many men take possession of a ' little city of sewers,' but I should think a pure and good woman might chance to find herself in the ' temple of the Holy Ghost.' "

His visitor was somewhat startled by this forcible language, and he did not answer for a moment. He seemed to be attentively studying the pattern of the carpet. Presently he looked full at Dudley, and spoke somewhat sharply.

"Knowing all you do, you think that possible?"

"Knowing all I do, I think that more than possible."

The man of the world sat for some time in silence, tapping his boot with a ruler he had taken from the writing-table.

"I'll tell you what I can do for you," said Dudley, suddenly. " I can give you the address of the Women's Medical School. Your niece is probably there."

" Oh Lord, no ! I am a brave man, but I am not equal to that. I would rather face a tiger in the jungle any day. Well, sir, I am sure

I am infinitely obliged to you. I wish I could ask you to dine at my club, but I hope I shall see you when I am next in London. That is my card. Where's the little chap? Look here, my man! There is a Christmas-box for you, but if you ever get under my horses' feet again, I will drive right on; do you hear?"

He shook hands cordially with Dudley, slipped a couple of guineas into his hand, and in another minute the impatient bays were dashing down the street.

" Sir Douglas Munro," said Dudley, examining the card. " A magnificent specimen of the fine old Anglo-Indian type. I should like to see this wonderful niece of his!"

CHAPTER XXXIV.

PALM-TREES AND PINES.

A WORLD of palm-trees and pines, of aloes and
eucalyptus, of luxuriant hedges all nodding and
laughing with gay red roses, of white villas
gleaming out from a misty background of olives,
of cloudless sky looking down on the deep blue
sea—a vivid sunshiny world, and in the midst
of it all, Miss Lucy, to all appearance as gay
and as light-hearted as if she had never dis-
sected the pterygo-maxillary region, nor pored
over the pages of Quain.

The band was playing waltzes in the garden
below, and Lucy, as she dressed, was dancing
and swaying to and fro, like the roses in the
wind.

"*Entrez!*" she cried, without moderating her
steps, as she heard a knock at the door.

It was Evelyn, fair, tall, and somewhat severe.

"You are not very like a medical student," she said, gravely.

"I should take that for an unmixed compliment, if I did not know what it meant."

"What does it mean?"

"That I am not in the least like Mona."

"Well, you are not, you know."

"True, *ma belle*. It was you who fitted on the lion's skin, not I. But did you come into my room just to tell me that?"

"I came to say that if you can be ready in ten minutes, Father will take us all to Monte Carlo."

"Ten minutes! Oh, Evelyn, and you have wasted one! What are you going to wear?"

"This, of course. What should I wear?"

Lucy selected a gown from her wardrobe. "But is not Sir Douglas still awfully tired with the journey?" she asked, looking over her shoulder to get a back view of her pretty skirt in the pier-glass.

"He has rested more or less for two days, and he is anxious to see the Monteiths before they go on to Florence."

She did not add, " I told him you were pining
to see Monte Carlo before you go home."

" The Monteiths," repeated Lucy, involuntarily. And as she heard the name on her own
lips, the healthy flush on her cheek deepened
almost imperceptibly.

Evelyn seated herself on a hat-box.

" I don't believe you will ever be a doctor,"
she remarked, calmly.

" What do you bet ? " Lucy did not look up
from the arduous task of fastening her bodice.

" I don't bet; but if you ever are, I'll—*consult*
you ! "

And having solemnly discharged this Parthian
dart, she left the room.

In truth, the two girls were excellent friends,
although they were continually sparring. Evelyn considered Lucy an absolute fraud in the
capacity of " learned woman," but she did not
on that account find the light-hearted medical student any the less desirable as a companion. As to comparing her with Mona, Evelyn would have laughed at the bare idea ; and
loyal little Lucy would have been the first to
join in the laugh : she had never allowed any
one even to suspect that she had passed an ex-

amination in which Mona had failed. Mona
was the centre of the system in which she was a
satellite ; she was bitterly jealous of all the other
satellites in their relation to the centre, but who
would be jealous of the sun ?

Lady Munro had taken a great fancy to her
visitor. She would not have owned to the
heresy for the world, but she certainly was much
more at her ease in Lucy's society than she ever
had been in Mona's, and how Sir Douglas could
find his niece more *piquante* than Lucy Reynolds, she could not even imagine. She knew
exactly where she had Lucy, but even when
Mona agreed with her most warmly, she had an
uncomfortable feeling that a glance into her
niece's mind might prove a little startling. She
met Lucy on common ground, but Mona seemed
to be on a different plane, and Lady Munro found
it extremely difficult to tell when that plane was
above, and when below, her own.

She would have been not a little surprised,
and her opinion of the relative attractions of the
two friends might have been somewhat altered,
had any one told her that Mona admired and
idealised her much more even than Lucy did.
If any one of us were unfortunate enough to

receive the "giftie" of which the poet has sung,
it is probable that the principal result of such
insight would be a complete readjustment of
our friendships.

But now Sir Douglas had appeared upon the
scene, and of course Lucy was much more
anxious to "succeed" with him than with either
of the others. She had seen very little of him
as yet, and she had done her best, but so far the
result had been somewhat disappointing. It
was almost a principle with Sir Douglas never
to pay much attention to a pretty young girl.
He had seen so many of them in his day, and
they were all so much alike. Even this saucy
little *Æsculapia militans* was no exception.
As the scientist traces an organism through " an
alternation of generations," and learns by close
observation that two or three names have been
given to one and the same being, so Sir Douglas fancied he saw in Lucy Reynolds only an
old and familiar type in a new stage of its
life-history.

He had gone through much trouble and perplexity on the subject of Mona's life-work ; and
Dudley's somewhat fanciful words had for the
first time given expression to a vague idea that

had floated formless in his own mind ever since he first met his niece at Gloucester Place. It would be ridiculous to apply such an explanation to Lucy's choice, but Sir Douglas had no intention of opening up the problem afresh. He took for granted that Lucy had undertaken the work "for the fun of the thing," because it was novel, startling, *outré;* and he confided to his wife that "that old Reynolds must be a chuckle-headed noodle in his dotage to allow such a piece of nonsense."

In a very short time after Evelyn's summons to Lucy, the whole party were rattling down the hill to the station, in the crisp, cold, dewy morning air. Evelyn was calm and dignified as usual, but Lucy was wild with excitement. Everything was a luxury to her—to be with a man of the world like Sir Douglas, to travel in a luxurious first-class carriage, to see a little bit more of this wonderful world.

They left Nice behind them, and then the scenery became gradually grander and more severe, till the train had to tunnel its way through the mighty battlements of rock that towered above the sea, and afforded a scanty nourishment to the scattered pines, all tossed and bent and twisted by the wind in the enervating climate of the south. At last, jutting out above the water, at the foot of the rugged heights, as though it too, forsooth, had the rights of eternal nature, Monte Carlo came in view,—gay, vulgar, beautiful, tawdry, irresistible Monte Carlo!

"Is that really the Casino?" said Lucy, in an eager hushed voice.

Sir Douglas laughed. Lucy's enthusiasm pleased him in spite of himself.

"It is," he said; "but, if you have no objection, we'll have something to eat before we visit it."

To him the Casino was a commonplace toy of yesterday; to Evelyn it was a shocking and beautiful place, that one ought to see for once; to Lucy it was a temple of romance. No need to bid her speak softly as she entered the gorgeous, gloomy halls, with their silent eager groups.

"Shall we see Gwendolen Harleth?" she whispered to Evelyn.

On this occasion, however, Gwendolen Harleth was conspicuous by her absence. There were a number of women at the roulette-tables who looked like commonplace, hard - working governesses; there were be-rouged and be-jewelled ladies of the *demi-monde*; there were wicked, wrinkled old harpies who always seemed to win; and there were one or two ordinary blooming young girls; but there was no Gwendolen Harleth. For a moment Lucy was almost disappointed. It all looked so like a game with counters, and no one seemed to care so very much where the wheel stopped: surely the tragedy of this place had been a little overdrawn.

At that instant her eyes fell on an English boy, whose fresh honest face was thrown into deep anxious furrows, and who kept glancing furtively round, as if to make sure that no one noticed his misery. His eye met Lucy's, and with a great effort he tried to smooth his face into a look of easy assurance. He was not playing, but he went on half unconsciously, jotting down the winning numbers on a slip of paper.

" *Messieurs, faites vos jeux.*"

The boy opened a large lean pocket-book, and drew out his last five-franc piece.

" *Le jeu est fait.*"

With sudden resolution he laid it on the table, and pushed it into place.

" *Rien ne va plus.*"

" *Vingt-sept.*"

And the poor little five-franc piece was swept into the bank.

The boy smiled airily, and returned the empty book to his pocket.

Lucy looked at her companions, but none of them had noticed the little tragedy. Sir Douglas led the way to another table, and finally he handed a five-franc piece to each of the girls. To his mind it was a part of the programme that they should be able to say they had tried their luck.

Lucy hesitated, strongly tempted. Dim visions floated before her mind of making " pounds and pounds," and handing them over to that poor boy. Then she shook her head.

" My father would not like it," she whispered.

Sir Douglas shrugged his shoulders. Verily, there was no accounting for taste. How a man could allow his daughter to spend years in the dissecting-room, and in the surgical wards of a hospital,—subject her, in fact, to the necessity of spending her life in an atmosphere of carbolic, — and object to her laying a big silver

counter on a green cloth, just for once, was
more than he could divine.

Evelyn hesitated also.   But it would be such
fun to say she had done it.   She took the coin
and laid it on the table.   "Where would you
put it?" she whispered rather helplessly to
Lucy.

Lucy knew nothing of the game, but she
had been watching its progress attentively, and
her eye had been trained to quick and close observation.   Annoyed at Evelyn's slowness, and
without stopping to think, she took the cue
and pushed the coin into place.   It was just in
time.   In another instant Evelyn's stake was
doubled.

"There, that will do," said Sir Douglas, as
Evelyn seemed inclined to repeat the performance.   "I don't want to see your cheeks like
those of that lady opposite."

A gentleman stood aside to let them leave the
table, and as they passed he held out his hand
to Lucy.   She did not take it at once, but
looked up at Sir Douglas in pretty conster-
nation.

"*There!*" she said.   "I knew it!   This is
one of my father's churchwardens."

Sir Douglas was much amused. "Well," he said, "you have at least met on common ground!"

Lucy attempted a feeble explanation of the situation in which she had been caught, and then hastily followed the others to the inner temples sacred to *Rouge et Noir*. Here, at least, there was tragedy enough even at the first glance. Lucy almost forgot the poor lad at the roulette-table, as she watched the piles of gold being raked hither and thither with such terrific speed. One consumptive-looking man, whose face scarcely promised a year of life, was staking wildly, and losing, losing, losing. At last the piles in front of him were all gone. After a moment's hesitation they were followed by note after note from his pocket-book. Then these too came to an end, but still the relentless wheel went on with that swiftness that is like nothing else on earth. The man made no movement to leave the table. With yellow-white shaking hands he continued to note the results, and while all the rest were staking and winning and losing, he went on aimlessly, feverishly pricking some meaningless design on the ruled sheet before him. And all the time two young girls were gaining, gaining, gaining, and smiling to the men behind them as they raked in the piles of gold.

"Let us go," said Lucy, quickly. "I cannot bear this."

"I do think we have had enough of it," Lady Munro agreed. "I am thirsty, Douglas; let us have some coffee."

They strolled out into the bright sunshine.

"Well," said Sir Douglas, "a little disappointing, *n'est ce pas?*"

"Oh no," said Lucy; "not at all. It is far more real than I thought. The only disappointing thing is that——"

"What?"

She lifted her eyes with an expression of profound gravity.

"All the women trim their own hats."

"Why, Lucy," put in Evelyn, "I saw some very nice hats."

"I did not say none of them trimmed their hats *well*," said Lucy, severely. "I only said they all trimmed their own."

"We are rather too early in the day for *toilettes*," said Sir Douglas. "I confess one does not see many attractive women here; but there was a highly respectable British matron just opposite us at that last table."

" Yes," said Lucy, indignantly. " She was the worst of all ; sailing about in her comfortable British plumage, with that air of self-satisfied horror at the depth of Continental wickedness, and of fond pride in the bouncing flapper at her heels. She made me feel that it was worse to look on than to play."

" Don't distress yourself," said Sir Douglas, quietly ; " you did play, you know. Ask the churchwarden."

" I owe you five francs," said Evelyn, "or ten. Which is it ? "

" *Don't !* " said Lucy. " It is no laughing matter for me, I can assure you. Many is the trick I have played on that man. Heigh-ho ! He has his revenge."

" Don't be down-hearted. You had at least the satisfaction of winning."

But Lucy was in no humour for being teased, and, to change the subject, she began to tell the story of the different tragedies she had witnessed.

" It is all nonsense, you know," said Sir Douglas, good-humouredly. " That is the sort of stuff they put in the good books. People who are really being bitten don't attract attention to themselves by overdone by-play."

Lucy did not reply, but she retained her own opinion. Overdone by-play, indeed! As if she had eyes for nothing more subtle than overdone by-play!

"In the meantime we will have our coffee," said Sir Douglas, "and then I will leave you at the concert, while I look up Monteith. I will come and fetch you at the end of the first part. Here, Maud, this table is disengaged."

The head-waiter came up immediately. Sir Douglas was one of those people who rarely have occasion to *call* a waiter. He gave the order, lighted a cigar very deliberately, and then turned abruptly to Lucy.

"Where is Mona?" he asked, quietly.

Lucy almost gasped for breath.

"She was in London when I saw her last," she said, trying to gain time.

"At her old rooms?"

"No-o," faltered Lucy. "She was sharing my rooms then."

Then she gathered herself together. This would never do. Anything would be better than to suggest that there was a mystery in the matter.

"You see," she said, "I have been away ever since the beginning of term, and I have not heard from Mona for some time. I know she has taken all the classes she requires for her next examination, and reading can be done in one place as well as in another."

"Then why the—why could not she come to us and do it?"

Lucy laughed. She began to hope that the storm was passing over.

"I suppose Mona would reply," she said, "that Cannes, like Cambridge, is an excellent place to play in."

"Then you don't know her address?"

"I don't know it positively. I think it is quite likely that she is with that cousin of hers in the north. She said once that she could do far more work in that bracing air."

"So she has gone there to prepare for this examination?"

"I believe she is working very hard."

"And when does the examination take place?"

"I have not heard her say when she means

to go up. You see, Sir Douglas, my plans are
Mona's, but Mona's plans are her own. She
is not one to rush through her course anyhow,
for the sake of getting on the register, like—
me for instance."

"I can believe that. It seems Mona told
her aunt that she was leaving her old rooms,
and that it would be well to address letters
for the present to the care of her man of business. Is that what you do?"

"I have not written for a long time. I shall
send my next to her man of business."

"And won't I just give Mona a vivid account
of how I came to do it!" she added, mentally.

"Have you seen this lady—Mona's cousin?
I don't know anything about her."

"No, I have not. I believe she is very quiet,
and elderly, and respectable,—and dull; the
sort of person in whose house one can get
through a lot of work."

"Humph," growled Sir Douglas. "A nice
life for a girl like Mona!"

"I am sure I wish she were here!"

Sir Douglas looked at her. "Some of us,"
he said, quietly, "wish that every day of our
lives. I called the other day to take her for a

drive in the Park, but found she had left her old rooms." And then he told the story of his little misadventure of a few days before.

"Oh," said Lucy, "what a terrible pity! Mona *loves* driving in the Park. Do go for her again some day when she is working in London. You have no idea what a treat a drive in the Park is to people who have been poring over their bones, and their books, and their test-tubes."

"Well, what in the name of all that is incomprehensible does she do it for? She might drive in the Park every day if she chose."

"But then," said Lucy, "she would not be Mona."

The muscles of his face relaxed, and then contracted again.

"Even admitting," he said, "that all is well just now, how will it be ten years hence?"

"Ten years hence," said Evelyn, "Mona will have married a clever young doctor. Lucy says the students have several times married the lecturers."

Sir Douglas frowned. "I should just like to see," he flashed out angrily, "the young doctor who would presume to come and ask me for

Mona! I hate the whole trade. Why, that young fellow I told you about, who came to my rescue, was infinitely superior to most of them—cultured, and travelled, and that sort of thing—but, bless my soul! he was not a man of the world. I would sooner see Mona in a convent than give her to a whipper-snapper like that!"

"Evelyn is wrong," said Lucy. "Mona will not marry. She never thinks of that sort of thing. Ten years hence she will be a little bit matronly, by reason of all the girls and women she will have mothered. Her face will be rather worn perhaps, but in my eyes at least she will be beautiful."

"And in yours, Douglas," said Lady Munro, "she will still be the bright young girl that she is to-day."

She laughed softly as she spoke, but the laugh was a rather half-hearted one. She had learnt the difference between the fruit that is in a man's hand, and the fruit that is just out of reach.

CHAPTER XXXV.

WEEPING AND LAUGHTER.

Sir Douglas had gone to see his friend, but it was still too early for the concert, so Lady Munro and the girls strolled round to the terrace overlooking the sea.

"How lovely, how lovely!" said Lucy. "I wonder if there is any view in all the world like this?"

"We must find those two statues by Sara Bernhardt and Gustave Doré," said Evelyn, looking up from her Baedeker. "One of them represents——"

"Oh, bother the statues!" cried Lucy. "I want to feel things to-day, not to look at them." Her voice changed suddenly. "Lady Munro," she said very softly, "that is my boy leaning on the stone balustrade. Now, did I exaggerate? Look at him!"

Lady Munro walked on for a moment or two, and then glanced at the lad incidentally; but the glance extended itself with impunity into a very deliberate study. The boy's face was flushed, and he was muttering to himself incoherently as he gazed in front of him with unseeing eyes.

"He looks as if he was going mad," remarked Evelyn, frankly.

"He looks a great deal more like an acute maniac than most acute maniacs do," said Lucy, with a proud recollection of a few visits to an asylum. "Oh, Lady Munro, do, do go and speak to him! You would do it so beautifully."

Lady Munro hesitated. She never went out of her way to do good, but this boy seemed to have come into her way; and her action was none the less beautiful, because it was dictated, not by principle at all, but by sheer motherly impulse.

She left the girls some distance off, and rustled softly up to where he stood.

"*Pardon, monsieur*," she said, lightly, "can you tell me where the statue by Gustave Doré is?"

He started and looked up. One did not

often see a gracious woman like this at Monte Carlo.

"I beg your pardon," he said, making a desperate effort to collect his thoughts. Distraught as was his air, his accent and manner were cultured and refined. Lady Munro's interest in him increased.

"Do you know where there is a statue by Gustave Doré?"

He shook his head. "I am sorry I don't," he said, and he turned away his face.

But Lady Munro did not mean the conversation to end thus. "This is a charming view, is it not?" she said.

"Ye-e-s," he said; "oh, very charming."

"I think I saw you at one of the tables in the Casino. I hope you were successful?"

He turned towards her like a stag at bay. There was anger and resentment in his face, but far more deeply written than either of these was despair. It was such a boyish face, too, so open and honest. "Don't you see I can't talk about nothings?" it seemed to say. "You are very kind and very beautiful; I am at your mercy; but why do you torture me?"

"You are in trouble," Lady Munro said, in

her soft, irresistible voice. "Perhaps it is not so bad after all. Tell me about it."

A woman more accustomed to missions of mercy would have calculated better the effect of her words. In another moment the tears were raining down the lad's cheeks, and his voice was choked with sobs. Fortunately, the great terrace was almost entirely deserted. Lucy and Evelyn sat at some distance, apparently deep in the study of Baedeker, and in a far-off corner an old gentleman was reading his newspaper.

The story came rather incoherently at last, but the thread was simple enough.

The boy had an only sister, a very delicate girl, who had been ordered to spend the winter at San Remo. He had taken her there, had seen her safely installed, and—had met an acquaintance who had persuaded him to spend a night at Monte Carlo on the way home. From that point on, of course, the story needed no telling. But the practical upshot of it was that the boy had in his purse, at that moment, precisely sixty-five centimes in money, and a twenty-five-centime stamp; he had nothing wherewith to pay the journey home, and he was some pounds in debt to his friend.

Truly, all things are relative in life. While some men were forfeiting their thousands at the tables with comparative equanimity, this lad was wellnigh losing his reason for the sake of some fifteen pounds.

"What friends had he at home?" was of course Lady Munro's first question. "Had he a father—a mother?"

His mother was dead, and his father—his father was very stern, and not at all rich. It had not been an easy matter for him to send his daughter to the Riviera.

"That is what makes it so dreadful," said the lad. "I wish to heaven I had taken a return ticket! but I wanted to go home by steamer from Marseilles. The fatal moment was when I encroached on my journey-money. After I had done that, of course I had to go on to replace it; but the luck was dead against me. Oh, if I could only recall that first five francs! If I could have foreseen this—but I meant——"

"You meant to win, of course," said Lady Munro, kindly.

The boy laughed shamefacedly, in the midst of his misery.

"Well, I think my punishment equals my

sin," he said. "I would gladly live on bread
and water for months, if I could undo two days
of my life. I keep thinking round and round
in a circle, till I am nearly mad. I *cannot*
write to my father, and yet what else can I
do?"

Lady Munro was silent for a few minutes
when the lad had finished speaking. She was
wondering what Sir Douglas would say. When
a married woman is called upon to help her
fellows, she has much to think of besides her
own generous impulses; and in Lady Munro's
case it was well perhaps that this was so. She
would empty her purse for the needy as readily
as she would empty it for some jewel that took
her fancy, sublimely regardless in the one case
as in the other of the wants of the morrow.
Ah, well! it is a good thing for mankind that
a perfect woman is not always essential to the
rôle of ministering angel!

"I will try to help you," she said at last,
"though I cannot absolutely promise. In
the meantime here is a napoleon. That will
take you to Cannes, and pay for a night's
lodging. Call on me to-morrow between ten
and eleven." She handed him her card. "I

think," she added as an afterthought, "you will promise not to enter the Casino again ?"

It was very characteristic of her to ask as a favour what she might have demanded as a condition. The boy blushed crimson as he took the napoleon. "You are very kind," he said, nervously. "Thank you. I won't so much as look at the Casino again."

"Well, Miss Lucy, a pretty scrape you have got me into!" said Lady Munro, as she joined the girls. "It will take fifteen pounds to set that boy on his feet again."

"Tell us all about it," said Lucy, eagerly. "Who is he ?"

"His name is Edgar Davidson, and he is a medical student."

"I knew it! No wonder I was interested in a brother of the cloth ! What hospital ?"

"I don't know."

"Is he going in for the colleges or for the university ?"

"My dear child, how should I think of asking ?"

"I suppose mother did not even inquire who his tailor was," said Evelyn, quietly.

"I don't mind about his tailor but it would

interest me to know where he gets his scalpels sharpened. What brings him here during term?"

Lady Munro had just time to give a sketch of the lad's story, when they arrived at the door of the concert-hall—wonderful alike for its magnificence and its vulgarity—to find the orchestra already carrying away the whole room with a brilliant, piquant, irresistible *pizzicato*.

"Do take a back seat, mother," whispered Evelyn; "we can't have Lucy dancing right up the hall."

Lucy shot a glance of lofty scorn at her friend.

"I am glad at least that Providence did not make me a lamp-post," she said, severely.

The last note of the piece had not died away, when a young man came forward and held out his hand to Lady Munro.

"Why, Mr Monteith, my husband has just gone to your hotel."

"Yes; he told me you were here, so I left him and my father together."

He shook hands with the two girls, and seated himself beside Lucy.

"You here?" she said, with an air of calm indifference, which was very unlike her usual impulsive manner.

"Nay, it is I who should say that. You here? And you leave me to find it out by chance from Sir Douglas?"

"It did not occur to me that you would be interested;" and she fanned herself very gracefully, but very unnecessarily, with her programme.

"Little coquette!" thought Lady Munro. But Lucy looked so charming at the moment, that not even a woman could blame her.

"How is Cannes looking?"

"Oh, lovely — lovelier than ever. Some awfully nice people have come."

"So you don't miss any of those who have gone?"

"Not in the least."

"And you would not care to see any old friend back again for a day or two?"

There was a moment's pause.

"I don't think there would be room; the hotel seems full——"

With a sudden burst of harmony the music began, and there was no more conversation till the next pause.

" Have you ever walked up to the chapel on the hill again ? "

" Oh, lots of times ! "

" You have been energetic. Have you chanced to see the Maritime Alps in the strange mystical light we saw that day ? "

" Yes. They always look like that."

" Curious ! Then I suppose the walk has no longer any associations——"

" Oh, but it has—bitter associations ! We left the path to get some asparagus, and my gown caught in a bramble-bush, and a dog barked——"

The first soft notes of the violins checked the tragic sequel of her tale, and the music swelled into a pathetic wailing waltz, which brought the first part of the programme to an end.

Sir Douglas came during the interval to take them away, and Mr Monteith walked down with them to the station.

" I am sorry there is no room for me at the hotel," he said, as he stood with Lucy on the platform.

" Pray, don't take my word for it. I don't ' run the shanty.' Perhaps you could get a bed."

" What is the use, if people would be sorry to see an old acquaintance ? "

" How can you say such things ? " said Lucy, looking up at him cordially. " I am sure there are some old ladies in the hotel who would be delighted to see you."

" But no young ones ? "

" I can't answer for them."

" You can for yourself."

" Oh yes."

" And you don't care one way or the other ? "

" No ; " she shook her head slowly and regretfully.

" Not at all ? "

" Not at all."

" Not the least bit in the world ? "

Lucy lifted her eyes again demurely. " When one comes to deal with such very small quantities, Mr Monteith," she said, " it is difficult to speak with scientific accuracy. If you really care to know——"

" Yes ? "

" Where are the Munros ? "

" In the next carriage. Do finish your sentence."

" I don't remember what I was going to say,"

said Lucy, calmly. "A sure proof, my old nurse used to tell me, that it was better unsaid."

She sprang lightly up the high step of the carriage, and then turned to say good-bye. The colour in her cheeks was very bright.

Ten minutes later she seemed to have forgotten everything except the wonderful afterglow, which reddened the rocks and trees, and converted the whole surface of the sea into one blazing ruby shield.

Sir Douglas was nodding over his newspaper. Lucy laid her hand on Lady Munro's soft fur.

"You have been very good to me," she said. "I don't know how to thank you. I really think you have opened the gates of Paradise to me."

The words suggested a meaning that Lady Munro did not altogether like, but she answered lightly,—

"It has been a great pleasure to all of us to have you, dear ; but you know we don't mean to let you go on Thursday."

Lucy smiled. "I must," she said, sadly. "A week hence it will all seem like a beautiful dream—a dream that will last me all my life."

"Well, I am glad to think the roses in your cheeks are no dream, and I hope they will last you all your life, too."

And then the careless words re-echoed through her mind with a deeper significance, and she wished Sir Douglas would wake up and talk, even if it were only to grumble.

That night there were two private conversations.

Evelyn had gone into Lucy's room to brush her hair in company.

"What a touching sight!" said Lucy, laughing suddenly, as, by the dancing firelight, she caught sight of the two fair young figures in the mirror—their loosened hair falling all about their shoulders. "Come on with your confidences! Now is the time. At least so they say in books."

"Unfortunately I have not got any confidences."

"Nor have I — thank heaven!" She bent low over the glowing wood-fire. "What slavery love must be!"

Evelyn watched her with interest, but Lucy's next words were somewhat disappointing.

"Evelyn," she said, "how is it Mona has contrived to charm your father so? I need not tell you what I think about her, but, broadly speaking, she is not a man's woman, and I should not have fancied she was the sort of girl to fetch Sir Douglas at all."

"I don't think it strange," said Evelyn, languidly. "I have often thought about it. You see, she is very like what my mother must have been at her age, though not nearly so charming to mere acquaintances; and then just where the dear old Mater stops short, the real Mona begins. It must be such a surprise to father!"

"That is ingenious, certainly. How Mr Monteith admires your mother!"

"Does he?"

"I wonder what he would think of Mona!"

"I can't guess."

"Have you known him long?"

"Father and Mother have known his father long."

"Do you think he is honest?"

"Which?"

"The son, of course."

"He never stole anything from me."

" Don't be a goose ! Do you think he means what he says ? "

Evelyn paused before replying.

" You don't ? " said Lucy, quickly.

" I was trying to remember anything he did say," Evelyn answered, very deliberately. " The only remark I can remember addressed to myself was, ' Brute of a day, isn't it ? ' I think he meant that. He certainly looked as if he did."

" Douglas," said Lady Munro, " would Colonel Monteith allow his son to marry Lucy Reynolds ? "

" Nonsense ! what ideas you do take into your head ! "

" Because, if he would not, things have gone quite far enough. George said something to me about coming back to Cannes for a day or two. Of course that child is the attraction. If you think it will end in nothing, he must not come."

" So that is what her vocation amounts to ! "

" My dear Douglas ! what does she know of life ? She is a child——"

" Precisely, and her father is another. God

bless my soul! Monteith's son must marry an heiress."

Lady Munro did not pursue the subject; she had something else to talk of. She rose presently, and walked across the room.

"Douglas," she said, stopping idly before the glass, "I wish you would give me your recipe for looking youthful. You will soon look younger than your wife."

"Nonsense," he said gruffly, but he smiled. His wife did not often make pretty speeches now-a-days. As it happened she was looking particularly young that night, too. Perhaps that fact had struck her, and had suggested the remark.

For half an hour they chatted together, as they might have done in the old, old days, and then——

And then Lady Munro broached the subject of the boy at Monte Carlo.

CHAPTER XXXVI.

NORTHERN MISTS.

IT seems gratuitously cruel to take my readers back to bleak old Borrowness in this dreary month of December; away from the roses and the sunshine, and the wonderful matchless blue, to the mud, and the mist, and the barren fields, and the cold, grey sea.

Princely, luxurious Cannes! Home of the wealth of nations! stretched out at ease like a beautiful woman, along the miles of wooded hill that embrace the bay. Homely, work-a-day Borrowness! stooping down all unseen, shrouded in northern mists, to gather its daily bread. Do you indeed belong to the same world? feel the same needs? share the same curse? Do the children play on the graves in the one as in the other? in both do man and maid touch hands

and blush and wonder? Is there canker at the
core of the luscious glowing fruit? is there
living sap in the heart of the gnarled and
stunted tree? Beautiful Cannes! resting, ex-
panding, enjoying, smiling! Brave little Borrowness! frowning and panting and sighing, and
wiping with weary hand the sweat from a work-
worn brow!

Christmas was drawing near, but it had been
heralded by no fairy frost, only by rain and fog
and dull grey skies. Mona's life had been
unmarked by any event that had distinguished
one day from another. The last entry in the
unwritten diary of her life was some three weeks
old, and consisted of one word in red letters—
Stradivarius. And yet the days had been so
full, that, in order to redeem her promise to Mr
Reynolds, she had often found herself constrained, when bedtime came, to rake together
the embers of the fire, and spend an hour over
the mechanics of the circulation, or the phe-
nomena of isomerism. "Don't talk to me of
the terpenes or the recent work on the sugars,"
she wrote to a friend in London, who had offered
to send her some papers. "I have little time to
read at all; and when I do, I have sworn to

keep to the beaten track. Well-thumbed, jog-
trot text-books for me; no nice damp Trans-
actions! Wae is me! wae is me! You must
send your entrancing fairy tales to some one
else!"

Trade had continued very brisk in the little
shop; indeed its character and reputation had
completely changed. A few interesting boxes
had arrived from the stores, and the local
traveller no longer had amusing tales to relate
of the way in which Miss Simpson kept shop.
In fact, had it not been for his prospects in life,
and for his desire to spare the feelings of his
family, he would have been strongly tempted to
offer his heart and hand to Miss Simpson's
bright and capable assistant. It would be an
advantage in many ways to have a wife who
understood the business; and, poor thing, she
would not readily find a husband in Borrowness.
She was thrown away at present—there was no
doubt of that. Why, with her quick head at
figures, and her fine lady manners, she could get
a situation anywhere.

Mona, fortunately, was all unaware of the
tempting fruit that dangled just above her head.
She had, it is true, some difficulty in keeping

the traveller to the point, when she had dealings
with him ; but her limited intercourse with the
other sex had not taught her to regard this as
peculiarly surprising.

What rejoiced her heart, far more even than
the success of the shop, was the number of
women and girls who had got into the way
of consulting her about all sorts of things. " I
exist here now," she wrote to Doris, " in the
dual capacity of assistant to Miss Simpson, and
of general referee on the choice of new goods
and the modification of old ones. 'Goods' is
a vague term, and is to be interpreted very
liberally. It includes not only dresses and
bonnets and furniture, but also husbands."

Rachel did not at all approve of this large
and unremunerative *clientèle.* If there had
been any question of " honesty and religion,
like," it would have been different ; but she
considered that the " hussies wasted a deal of
Mona's time, when she might have been better
employed."

To Matilda Cookson, of course, she objected
less ; but she never could sufficiently express
her wonder at Mona's inconsistency in this
respect.

"As soon as the Cooksons begin to notice you, you just bow down like all the rest, for all your fine talk," she said one day, in a moment of irritation.

Mona strove to find a gentle reply in vain, so, contrary to all her principles, she was constrained to receive the remark in irritating silence.

Matilda Cookson had remained very true to her allegiance, and would at this time have proved an interesting study to any psychologist whose path she had chanced to cross. Almost at a glance he could have divided all the opinions she uttered into two classes—those that were her own, and those that were Mona's. The former were expressed with timid deference ; the latter were flung in the face of her acquaintances, with a dogmatic air of finality that was none the less irritating because the opinions themselves were occasionally novel and striking. Matilda glowed with pride when she repeated a bold and original remark ; she stammered and blushed when one of her own poor fledgelings stole into the light. It was on the former that a rapidly developing reputation for "cleverness" was insecurely based ; it was the latter that

delighted Mona's heart, and made her intercourse with the girl a source of never-ceasing
interest. It is so easy to heap fuel on another
mind ; but to apply the first spark, to watch it
flicker, and glow, and catch hold—that is one of
the things that is worth living for.

To one of Mona's *protégées* Rachel never even
referred, and that was the girl who had fainted
at the *soirée*. Mona had taken an interest in
her patient, had prescribed a course of arsenic
and green vegetables ; and the improvement
in the girl's appearance had seemed almost
miraculous.

"She usedna tae be able tae gang up the
stair, without sittin' doon tae get her breath,"
said her grandmother to Miss Simpson one day;
" an' noo, my word ! she's awa' like a cat up a
tree."

Rachel carefully refrained from repeating this
remark to Mona. She was afraid that so surprising a result might encourage her cousin to
persevere in a work which Rachel fondly hoped
had been relinquished for ever. The good soul
had been much depressed on chancing to see
the prescription which Mona had written for
the girl. Why, it was a real prescription—like

one of Dr Burns'! When a woman had got the length of writing *that*, what was the use of telling her she would never make a doctor? What more, when you came to think of it, did doctors do? There was nothing for it but to encourage Mr Brown, and Rachel forthwith determined to invite him and his sisters to tea.

The study of the *Musci*, *Algæ*, and *Fungi* had not proved a striking success hitherto. There had been one delightful ramble among the rocks and pools, but since then the pursuit had somewhat flagged. Several excursions had been arranged, but all had fallen through. On one occasion Miss Brown had been confined to the house; on another she had been obliged to visit an aunt who was ill; and on a third the weather had been unpropitious.

"My dear," said Rachel one day, after the formation of the bold resolution above recorded, "if you are going in to Kirkstoun, you might stop at Donald's on the Shore, and order some cookies and shortbread. To-morrow's the day the cart comes round, and I'm expecting Mr Brown and his sisters to tea."

Mona nearly dropped the box of tape she was holding.

"Dear cousin," she said, "the sisters have never called on you, have they?"

"No," replied Rachel, frankly, "but one must make a beginning. They offered us tea the day we were there."

"I promised Mrs Ewing that I would play the organ for the choir practice to-morrow evening."

"Well, I'm sure I never heard the like! She just takes her use of you."

"You must not forget that she allows me to practise on the organ whenever I like. It is an infinite treat to me."

"And what's the use of it, I wonder? You can't take an organ about with you when you go out to tea."

"That's perfectly true," said Mona, laughing; "it is a selfish pleasure, no doubt."

"It all comes of your going to the English chapel in the evening. If you'd taken my advice, you'd never have darkened its doors. They say so much about Mr Ewing being a gentleman, but I do think it was a queer-like thing their asking you to lunch, and never saying a word about me. Mr Stuart doesn't set himself up for anything great, but he did ask you to tea along with me."

"The Ewings have not been introduced to you, dear."

"And whose doing is that, I'd like to know? We've met them often enough in the town."

Mona sighed. She considered that lunch at the Ewings' the great mistake of her life at Borrowness. She had resolved so heroically that Rachel's friends were to be her friends; but the invitation had been given suddenly, and she had accepted it. She had not stopped to think of infant baptism, or the relations of Church and State; or the propriety of a clergyman eking out his scanty stipend by raising prize poultry, or of allowing himself to be "taken up" by the people at the Towers; she had had a momentary mental vision of silky damask and of sparkling crystal, of intelligent conversation and of cultured voices, and the temptation had proved irresistible. The meek man lives in history by his hasty word, the truthful man's lie echoes on throughout the ages; the sin that is in opposition to our character, and to the resolutions of a lifetime, stands out before all the world with hideous distinctness. So in the very nature of things, if Mona had gone to Borrowness, as she might have done, armed with introductions to

all the county families in the neighbourhood,
Rachel would have felt herself less injured than
by that single lunch at the Ewings'.

" Well, I will order the things at Donald's,"
said Mona, after an awkward silence.

" Yes ; tell him I'll take the shortbread in any
case, but I'll only take the cookies if my visitors
come."

" Oh, then they have not accepted yet ? "

" No."

" Then I need not have distressed myself,"
thought Mona, " for they certainly won't come."
But she was annoyed all the same that Rachel
should have subjected herself to the unnecessary
snub of a refusal.

The refusal arrived that evening. It was
worded with bare civility. They " regretted
that they were unable," but they did not think
it necessary to explain why they were unable.

Rachel was very cross about the slight to herself, but she was not at all disheartened about
her plan. One trump-card was thrown away,
but she still held the king and the ace ; the king
was Mona's " tocher," and the ace was Mr Brown
himself. The original damp box of plants had
been followed by a number of others, and these

had latterly been hailed by Rachel with much
keener delight than they had afforded to Mona.
Mr Brown was all right; there could be no
shadow of doubt about that; and Rachel would
not allow herself to fancy for a moment that
Mona might be so blind to a sense of her own
interests as to side with the Misses Brown.

CHAPTER XXXVII.

THE ALGÆ AND FUNGI.

THE bazaar as an institution is played out.
There can certainly be no two opinions about
that.   It has lived through a youth of humble
usefulness, a middle life of gorgeous magnificence, and it is now far gone in an old age of
decrepitude and shams.   It has attained the
elaboration and complexity which are incompatible with farther existence, and it must die.
The cup of its abuse and iniquities is full.   It
has had its day ; let it follow many things better
than itself—great kingdoms, mighty systems—
into the region of the things that have been and
are not.

Yet even where the bazaar is already dead,
we all seem to combine, sorely against our will,
to keep the old mummy on its feet.   Nor is the

reason for our inconsistency far to seek. The
bazaar *knows its world ;* there is scarcely a
human weakness—a weakness either for good or
for evil—to which it does not appeal ; so it dies
hard, and, in spite of ourselves, we cherish it to
the last.

How we hate it ! How the very appearance
of its name in print fills our minds with reminiscences of nerve-strain, and boredom, and
shameless persecution !

This being so, it is a matter of profound regret to me that a bazaar should appear at all in
the pages of my story ; but it is bound up in-
extricably with the course of events, so I must
beg my readers to bear up as best they may.

" My dear," said Rachel, coming into the
shop one day, eager and breathless, " I have got
a piece of news for you to-day. The Miss
Bonthrons want you to help them with their
stall at the bazaar ! It seems they have been
quite taken with your manner in the shop, and
they think you'll be far more use than one
of those dressed-up fusionless things that only
want to amuse themselves, and don't know
what's left if you take three-and-sixpence from
the pound. Of course they are very glad, too,

that you should have the ploy. I told them
I was sure you would be only too delighted.
They were asking if there was no word of your
being baptised and joining the church yet."

Mona bent low over her account-book, and it
was a full minute before she replied. Her first
impulse was to refuse the engagement altogether ; her second was to accept with an indig-
nant protest ; her third and last was to accept
without a word. If she had been doomed to
spend a lifetime with Rachel, things would have
been different ; as it was, there were not three
more months of the appointed time to run. For
those months she must do her very utmost to
avoid all cause of offence.

" I think a bazaar is the very last thing I am
fitted for," she said, quietly ; "but, if you have
settled it with the Bonthrons, I suppose there is
nothing more to be said."

" Oh, you'll manage fine, I'm sure. There's
no doubt you've a gift for that kind of thing.
I can tell you there's many a one would be glad
to stand in your shoes. You'll see you'll get all
your meals in the refreshment-room for nothing,
and a ticket for the ball as well."

" I don't mean to go the ball."

" Hoots, lassie, you'll never stay away when the ticket costs you nothing ! I am thinking I might go myself, perhaps, to take care of you, like. It'll be a grand sight, they say, and it's not often I get the chance of wearing my green silk."

Again the infinite pathos of this woman, with all her vulgar, disappointed little ambitions, took Mona's heart by storm, as it had done on the night of her arrival at Borrowness ; and a gentle answer came unbidden to her lips.

That afternoon, however, she considered herself fully entitled to set off and drink tea with Auntie Bell, and Rachel raised no objection when she suggested the idea.

" I would be glad if you would do a little business for me, as you pass through Kilwinnie," she said.

" I will, with pleasure."

" Just go into Mr Brown's," she said, " and ask him if he still has green ribbon like what he sold me for my bonnet last year. The strings are quite worn out. I think a yard and a half should do. I'll give you a pattern."

Mona fervently wished that the bit of business could have been transacted in any other shop, but it would not do to draw back from her promise now.

As she passed along the high street of Kilwinnie, she saw Miss Brown's face at the window above the shop, and she bowed as she crossed the street. Mr Brown was engaged with another customer, so Mona went up to the young man at the opposite counter, thankful to escape so easily. But it was no use. In the most barefaced way Mr Brown effected an exchange of customers, and came up to her, his solemn face all radiant with sudden pleasure. His eyes, like those of a faithful dog, more than atoned at times for his inability to speak.

"How is Miss Simpson?" he asked. This was his one idea of making a beginning.

"She is very well, thank you," and Mona proceeded at once with the business in hand.

They had just settled the question, when, to Mona's infinite relief, Miss Brown tripped down the stair leading into the shop.

"Won't you come up-stairs and rest for ten minutes, Miss Maclean?" she said. "We are having an early cup of tea. No, no, Philip, we don't want you. Gentlemen have no business with afternoon tea."

Mona could not have told what induced her to accept the invitation. She certainly did not wish to do it. Perhaps she was glad to escape on any terms from those pathetic brown eyes.

Mr Brown's face fell, then brightened again.

"Perhaps while you are talking, you will arrange for another walk," he said.

Mona followed Miss Brown up the dark little stair into the house, and they entered the pleasant sitting-room. The ladies of the house received their visitor cordially, and proceeded to entertain her with conversation, which seemed to be friendly, if it was neither *spirituel* nor very profound. Presently it turned on the subject of husband-hunting.

"Now, Miss Maclean," said one, "would you call my brother an attractive man?"

Mona was somewhat taken aback by the directness of the question.

"I never thought of him in that connection," she answered, honestly.

"Well, you know, he is not a marrying man at all. Anybody can see that; and yet you would not believe me if I were to tell you the number of women who have set their caps at him. Any other man would have his head turned completely; but he never seems to see it. We get the laugh all to ourselves."

"Clever as he is," put in another sister, "he is a regular simpleton where women are concerned. He treats them just as if they were men, and of course they take advantage of it, and get him talked about and laughed at."

"We tell him it really is too silly," said the third, "that, after all his experience, he should not know how to take care of himself."

Mona turned very pale, but she answered thoughtfully.

"When you asked me whether I considered Mr Brown an attractive man, I was inclined at first to say no; but what you say of him crystallises my ideas somewhat. I think his great attraction lies in the fact that he can meet women on common ground, without regard to sex. He realises, perhaps, that a woman may care for knowledge, and even for friendship, as well as for a husband. I should not try to change him, if I were you. His views may be peculiar here, but they are not altogether uncommon among cultured people."

She said the last words gently, with a pleasant smile, and then proceeded to put on her furs with an air of quiet dignity that would not have discredited Lady Munro herself, and that seemed to throw the Browns to an infinite distance.

It was some moments before any of them found voice.

" Must you go ? " said the eldest at last, somewhat feebly. " Won't you take another cup of tea ? "

" Thank you very much, but I am on my way to drink tea with Mrs Easson."

" Queer homely body, isn't she ? " said the second sister, recovering herself. " She is your cousin, is she not ? "

" I am proud to say she is."

" Oh, we've never arranged about the walk," said the youngest. " Any day next week that will suit you, will suit me."

" Oh, thank you ; I am afraid this wonderful bazaar is going to absorb all our energies for some time to come. I fear the walk will have to be postponed indefinitely."

She shook hands graciously with her hostesses, and went slowly down by the stair that opened on the street.

" If I were five years younger," she said to herself, " I should be tempted to encourage Mr

Brown, just the least little bit in the world, and then——"

But not even when Mona was a girl could she have been tempted, for more than a moment, to avenge a petty wrong at the expense of those great, sad eyes.

Mr Brown had been looking out, and he came forward to meet her, nervous, eager.

"Have you arranged a day?" he asked.

"No; I fear I am going to be very busy for the next few weeks. It is very kind of you to suggest another walk. Good-bye."

She was unconscious that her whole manner and bearing had changed in the last quarter of an hour, but he felt it keenly, and guessed something of what had happened.

"Miss Maclean," he said, hoarsely, grasping the hand she tried to withdraw, "what do we want with one of them in our walks? Come with me. Come up-stairs with me now, and we'll tell them——"

"I have stayed too long already," said Mona, hastily; "good-bye." And without trusting herself to look at him again, she hurried away.

Her cheeks were very bright, and her eyes suffused with tears, as she continued her walk.

"How disgraceful!" she kept repeating; "how disgraceful! I must have been horribly to blame, or it never would have come to this."

But, as usual, before long her sense of the comic came to her rescue.

"Verily, my dear," she said, with a heavy sigh, "the study of the *Algæ* and *Fungi* is a large one, and leads us farther than we anticipated."

Auntie Bell would not have been the shrewd woman she was, if she had not seen at a glance that something was wrong with her darling; but she showed her sympathy by hastily "masking the tea," and cutting great slices from a home-made cake.

"Eh, but ye're a sicht for sair een! she said, as she bustled in and out of the sitting-room. "I declare ye're bonnier than iver i' that fur thing. Weel, hoo's a' wi' ye?"

"Oh, I am blooming, as you see. Rachel is well, too."

"An' what w'y suld she no' be weel? She's no i' the w'y o' daein' onything that's like to mak' her ill, I fancy, eh? Hae ye been efter the butterflies again wi' Maister Broon?"

The unexpected question brought the tell-tale colour to Mona's cheek.

"No," she said, "I am not going any more. It is not the weather for that sort of thing."

"Na," said Auntie Bell, tersely; "nor he isna the mon for that sort o' thing. He's a guid mon, nae doot, an' a cliver, they say, for a' he's sae quite an' sae canny, an' sae ta'en up wi's beasts and things; but he's no' the mon for the like o' you. Ye wadna tak' him, Mona?"

"Dear Auntie Bell," said Mona, abashed, "such a thing never even occurred to me——"

She did not add "until," but her honest face said it for her.

"He's no' been askin' ye?"

"No, no," said Mona, warmly, "and he never will. Can a man and woman not go 'after the butterflies,' as you call it, without thinking of love and marriage?"

Auntie Bell's face was worth looking at.

"I nae ken," she said, grimly; "I hae ma doots."

"Well, I assure you Mr Brown has not even mentioned such a thing to me."

Auntie Bell eyed her keenly through the gold spectacles, but Mona did not flinch.

"Then his sisters have," thought the old woman, shrewdly. "I'll gie them a piece o' ma mind the neist time I'm doun the toun."

Mona's visits were necessarily very short on these winter afternoons, and as soon as tea was over she rose to go.

"Are ye aye minded tae gang hame come Mairch?" said Auntie Bell.

"Oh yes, I cannot possibly stay longer."

"What's to come o' the shop?"

"I will look out for an intelligent young person to fill my place."

"Ay, ye may luik! Weel, I'll no' lift a finger tae gar ye bide. Yon's no' the place for ye. But I nae ken hoo I'm tae thole wi'oot the sicht o' yer bonny bricht een."

"Dear Auntie Bell," said Mona, affectionately, "you are coming to see me, you know."

"Me! hoot awa', lassie! It's a far cry tae Lunnon, an' I'm ower auld tae traivel ma lane."

They were standing by the open door, and the moonlight fell full on the worn, eager face.

"Then come with me when I go. I can't tell you how pleased and proud I should be to have you."

The old woman's face beamed. "Ay? My

word! an' ye'd tak' me in a first-cless cair-
riage, and treat me like a queen, I'll be boun'.
Mrs Dodds o' the neist fairm is aye speirin'
at me if I'll no' gang wi' the cheap trip tae
Edinbury for the New Year. I'll tell her I
could gang a' the w'y tae Lunnon, like a
leddy, an' no' be the puirer for the ootin' by ae
bawbee."

She executed a characteristic war-dance in the
moonlight. "Aweel," she resumed, with sudden
gravity, "ye'll mind me tae Rachel, and tell her
auld Auntie Bell's as daft as iver!"

"Well, you promised to dance at my wedding,
you know," and, waving her hand, Mona set off
with a light, quick step.

Her thoughts were very busy as she hastened
along, but her decision was made before she
reached home. "I will write a short note to
Mr Brown to-night," she said, "and tell him I
find life too short for the study of the *Algæ*
and *Fungi*."

CHAPTER XXXVIII.

THE BAZAAR.

IT was the first day of the bazaar.

The weather was mild and bright, and the whole town wore an aspect of excitement. The interior of the hall was not perhaps a vision of artistic harmony; the carping critic might have seen in it a striking resemblance to the brilliant, old-fashioned patchwork quilt which some good woman had sent as her contribution, and which was now being subjected to a fire of small wit and adverse criticism, in the process of being raffled; but, to the inhabitants of the place, such a sight was worth crossing the county to behold, and indeed, at the worst, it was a bright and festive scene with its brave bunting and festoons of evergreens.

"Let Kirkstoun flourish!" was inscribed in letters of holly along the front of the gallery,

in which a very fair brass band, accustomed
apparently to performing in the open air, was
pouring forth jaunty and dashing national
music, which fell with much acceptance on
well-balanced nerves.

The bazaar had formally been declared open
by the great local patron, Sir Roderick Allison
of Balnamora, and already the crowd was so
great that movement was becoming difficult.
Whatever Mona's feelings had been before the
" function " came on, she was throwing herself
into it now with heart and soul. All the day
before she had been hard at work, draping,
arranging, vainly attempting to classify; and
the Bonthrons had many times found occasion
to congratulate themselves on their choice of
an assistant. The good ladies had very shyly
offered to provide her with a dress for the
occasion, — " something a little brighter, you
know, than that you have on ; not but what
that's very nice and useful."

"Thank you very much," Mona had replied,
frankly. " I should be very glad to accept your
kind offer, but I have something in London
which I think will be suitable. I will ask a
friend to send it."

So now she was looking radiant, in a gown that was quiet enough too in its way, but which was so obviously a creation that it excited the attention of every one who knew her.

"She *does* look a lady!" said the Miss Bonthron with the eyeglass.

"Well, my dear," replied the one with the curls, "she might have *been* a lady, if her father had lived. They say he was quite a remarkable man, like his father before him. Where would we be ourselves if Father had not laid by a little property? I suppose it is all ordained for the best."

"I call it simply ridiculous for a shop-girl to dress like that," said Clarinda Cookson to her sister. "It is frightfully bad taste. Anybody can see that she never had on a dress like that in her life before. She means to make the most of this bazaar. It is a great chance for her."

Matilda bit her lip, and did not answer. By dint of long effort, silence was becoming easier to her.

And now none of the stall-holders had any leisure to think of dress, for this was the time of day when the people come who are really prepared to buy, independently of the chance of

a bargain ; and money was pouring in. Mona
was hard at work, making calculations for her
patronesses, hunting for " something that would
do for a gentleman," sympathising with the
people who were strongly attracted by a few,
and a few things only, on her stall, and those
the articles that were ticketed " sold,"—striving,
in short, for the moment, to be all things to
all men.

She felt that day as if she had received a
fresh lease of youth. Nothing came amiss to
her. She was the life and soul of her corner of
the hall, much to the delight of Doris, who,
fair, serene, and sweet, was watching her friend
in every spare moment from the adjoining stall.
Perhaps the main cause conducing to Mona's
good spirits was the fact that Rachel was confined to the house with a cold. Mona was
honestly and truly sorry for her cousin's disappointment ; she would gladly have borne the
cold and confinement vicariously ; but as that
was impossible—well, it was pleasant for a day
or two to be responsible only for her bright
young self.

In a surprisingly short time the ante-prandial
rush was over, and there was a comparative

lull, during which stall-holders could compare triumphant notes, or even steal away to the refreshment-room. But now there was a sudden stir and bustle at the door.

"Well, I declare," exclaimed Miss Bonthron, eagerly, "if this is not the party from the Towers!"

The two great local magnates of the neighbourhood were Sir Roderick Allison of Balnamora and Lord Kirkhope of the Towers. Sir Roderick, in his capacity of member for the eastern part of the county, took an interest in all that went on in the place; and although his presence at public gatherings was always considered a great honour, it was treated very much as a matter of course. The Kirkhopes, on the other hand, lived a frivolous, fashionable, irresponsible life; acknowledged no duties to their social inferiors, and were content to show their public spirit by permitting an occasional flower-show in their grounds; so, if on any occasion they did go out of their way to grace a local festivity, their presence was considered an infinitely greater triumph than was that of good bluff Sir Roderick. The parable of the prodigal son is of very wide application; and, where humanity only is concerned, its interpretation is sometimes a very sinister one.

Lady Kirkhope had filled her house with a large party of people for the Christmas holidays; and some sudden freak had induced her to bring a number of them in to the Kirkstoun Bazaar, just as a few months earlier she had taken her guests to the fair at St Rules, to see the fat woman and the girl with two heads. "Anything for a lark!" she used to say, and it might have been well if all the amusements with which she sought to while away her sojourn in the country had been as rational as these. As it was, good, staid country-people found it a little difficult sometimes to see exactly wherein the "lark" consisted. Even this fact, however, tended rather to increase than to diminish the excitement with which the great lady's arrival was greeted at the bazaar.

Mona, not being a native, was but little interested in the new-comers, save from a money-making point of view; and she was leaning idly against the wall, half smiling at the commotion the event had caused, when all at once her heart gave a leap, and the blood rushed madly over her face. Within twenty yards of

her, in Lady Kirkhope's party, chatting and
laughing, as he used to do in the good old days,
stood the Sahib. There was no doubt about it.
A correct morning dress had taken the place
of the easy tweeds and the old straw hat, but
the round, brotherly, boyish face was the same
as ever. The very sight of it called up in
Mona's mind a flood of happy reminiscences, as
did the friendly face of the moon above the
chimney-pots to the home-sick author of *Bilderbuch*.

Oh, it was good to see him again! For one
moment Mona revelled in the thought of all
they would have to say to each other, and
then——

"My dear," said Miss Bonthron, "I think
you have some little haberdashery-cases like
this in your shop. How much do you think we
might ask for it?"

Like the "knocking at the door in *Mac-
beth*," the words brought Mona back to a world
of prose realities. With swift relentless force
the recollection rushed upon her mind that the
Sahib had come with the "county people" to
honour the bazaar with his presence; while she
was a poor little shop-girl, who had been asked

to assist, partly as a great treat, and partly because of her skill in subtracting three-and-sixpence from the pound.

"Half-a-crown we price them. I think you might say three shillings here," she said, smiling; but deep down in her mind she was thinking, "Oh, I hope, I hope he won't notice me! Doris is bad enough, but picture the Sahib in the shop!" She broke into a little laugh that was half a sob, and her eyes looked suspiciously bright.

"Mona," said Doris, coming up to her suddenly, "somebody is looking very charming to-day, do you know?"

"Yes," said Mona boldly, flashing back the compliment in an admiring glance; "I have been thinking so all morning, whenever intervening crowds allowed me to catch a glimpse of her."

"I have been longing so to say to all the room, 'Do you see that bright young thing? She is a medical student!'"

"Pray don't!" said Mona, horrified. "My cousin would never forgive you—nor, indeed, for the matter of that, should I. How are you getting on?"

"My dear," was the reply, "I have sold more

rubbish this morning than I ever even saw before. After all, the secret of success at bazaars lies solely in the fact that there is *no* accounting for taste!"

At this moment a customer claimed Mona's attention, and, when she looked up again, Doris was in earnest conversation with an elderly gentleman. Mona overheard something about " women's power."

" Women," was the reply, delivered with a courteous bow, " have no power, they have only influence."

Doris flushed, then said serenely, " We won't dispute it. Influence is the soul, of which power is the outward form."

How sweet she looked as she stood there, her flower-like face uplifted, her dimpled chin in air, shy yet defiant! Mona thought she had never seen her friend look so charming, so utterly unlike everybody else. A moment later she perceived that she was not alone in her admiration. Unconscious that he was observed, a man stood a few yards off, listening to the conversation with a comical expression of amused, admiring interest; and that man was the Sahib.

Take your eyes off him, Mona, Mona, if you do not wish to be recognised! Too late! A wave of sunlight rushed across his face, kindling his homely features into a glow that gladdened Mona's heart, and swept away all her hesitation. Verily she could trust this man, whom all women looked upon as a brother.

He resolutely dismissed the sunshine from his face, however, as he came up and shook hands. He could not deny that he was glad to see her, but nothing could alter the fact that she had treated him very badly.

"I called on you in London," he said in an injured tone, after their first greetings had been exchanged, "but it was a case of 'Gone; no address.'"

"Oh, I am sorry," said Mona. "It never occurred to me that you would call."

He looked at her sharply. Her regret was so manifest that he could not doubt her sincerity; and yet it was difficult sometimes to believe that she was not playing fast and loose. It was not as if she were an ordinary girl, ready to flirt with any man she' met. Was it likely, after all they had said to each other in Norway, that he would let her slip out of his life without a protest? Was it possible that the idea of his calling upon her in London had never crossed her mind?

Mona was very far from guessing his thoughts. Strong in the conviction that she was not a "man's woman," she expected little from men, and counted little on what they appeared to give. She had a feeling of warm personal friendship for the Sahib, but it had never occurred to her to wonder what his feeling might be for her. Had they met after a separation of ten years, she would have welcomed with pleasure the cordial grasp of his hand; but that in the meantime he should go out of his way to see her, simply, as she said, never crossed her mind.

"Who would have thought of meeting you at a bazaar?" he said.

"It is I who should have said that. But, in truth, I am not here by any wish of my own. The arrangement was made for me. I should have looked forward to it with more pleasure if I had known I was to meet you."

His face brightened. "It is my turn now to protest that it is I who should have said that! My hostess brought a party of us. I am helping to spend Christmas in the old style at the Towers. Where are you staying, or have you just come over for the function?"

Mona's heart sank. "No; I am visiting a cousin in the neighbourhood."

"Then I hope I may give myself the pleasure of calling. Have you had lunch?"

"Not yet."

"That is right. I am sure you can be spared for the next quarter of an hour."

Mona introduced him to Miss Bonthron as a "family friend," and then took his arm. Now that they had met, no ridiculous notions of propriety should prevent their seeing something of each other.

"Do you know Lady Kirkhope?" he asked, as he piloted the way through the hall.

"No. I had better tell you at once that I am not in the least likely to know her; I——"

"Lady Kirkhope," said the Sahib suddenly, stopping in front of a vivacious dame, "I am sure you will be glad to make the acquaintance of Miss Maclean. She is the daughter of Gordon Maclean, of whom we were talking last evening."

"Then I am proud to shake hands with her," said the lady, graciously. "There are very few men, Miss Maclean, whom I admire as I did your father."

A few friendly words followed, and then the Sahib and Mona continued their way.

"Oh, Mr Dickinson," said Mona, when they had reached the large refreshment - room, and were seated in a deserted corner, "what *have* you done?"

"Well, what have I done?" said the Sahib, in good-humoured mystification. "I ought to have asked your permission before introducing you in a place like this; but Lady Kirkhope is not at all particular in that sort of way, and we met her so *à propos*. I am sure you would not mind if you knew how she spoke of your father."

"It is not that." Mona drew a long breath. "It is not your fault in the least, but I don't think any human being was ever placed in such a false position as I am." She hesitated. When she had first seen the glad friendly smile on the Sahib's face, she had fancied it would be so easy to tell him the whole story; but now the situation seemed so absurd, so grotesque, so impossible, that she could not find words.

"Mr Dickinson," she said at last, "Lady Munro really is my aunt."

"She appears to be under a strong impression to that effect."

"And Gordon Maclean was my father."

"So I have heard."

"And my mother, Miss Lennox, was a lady whom any one would have been glad to know."

"That I can answer for!"

"But I never told you all that? I never traded on my relatives, or even spoke of them?"

"I scarcely need to answer that question. Your exordium is striking, but don't keep me in suspense longer than you can help."

Mona did not join in his smile.

"All that," she said with a great effort, "is true; and it is equally true that at the present moment I am living with a cousin who keeps a small shop at Borrowness. I have been asked to sell at this bazaar simply because — *c'est mon métier, à moi.* I ought to do it well. Now you know why I did not wish to be introduced to Lady Kirkhope."

It was a full minute before the Sahib spoke, and then his answer was characteristic.

"What on earth," he asked, "do you do it for?"

Mona was herself again in a moment.

"Why do I do it?" she said, proudly. "Why should I not do it? My cousin has as much claim on me as the Munros have, and she needs me a great deal more. If I must stand or fall by my relatives, I choose to fall with Rachel Simpson rather than to stand with Lady Munro."

She rose to go, but he caught her hand.

"You said once that you had no wish to measure your strength against mine," he said, in a low voice. "I don't mean to let you go, so perhaps you had better sit down. It would be a pity to have a scene."   •

"Let my hand go in any case."

"Honest Injun?"

She yielded unwillingly with a laugh.

"Honest Injun," she said. "As we are here, I will stay for ten minutes," and she laid her watch on the table.

"That is right. I never knew any difficulty that was made easier by refusing to eat one's lunch."

"I don't admit that I am in any difficulty, and your way, too, is clear." She made a movement of her head in the direction of the door. "I am only sorry that you did not give me a

chance to tell you all this before you introduced
me to Lady Kirkhope. If I had known you
were coming, I should have given you a hint to
avoid me."

"Miss Maclean," he said, "will you allow me
to say that you are a little bit morbid?"

She met his eyes with a frank full glance from
her own.

"That is true," she said, with sudden conviction.

"And for a woman like you to see that you
are morbid is to cease to be morbid."

"I am sure I don't want to be; but indeed it
is so difficult to see what is simple and right. I
have often smiled to think how I told you in
summer, that the 'great, puzzling subject of com-
promise' had never come into my life."

"You said on the same occasion, if I remember
rightly, that my life was infinitely franker and
more straightforward than yours. I presume
you don't say so still?"

"I do, with all my heart."

"H'm. Do you think it likely that I would
go routing up poor relations for the pleasure of
devoting myself exclusively to their society?"

Mona's face flushed. "Mr Dickinson," she

said, "I ought to tell you that I arranged to come to my cousin before I met the Munros. I don't say that I should not have done it in any case, but I made the arrangement at a time when, with many friends, I was practically alone in the world. And also,"—she thought of Colonel Lawrence's story,—"even apart from the Munros, if I had known all that I know now, about circumstances in the past, I am not sure that I should have come at all. That is all my heroics are worth."

"You are a magnificently honest woman."

"I am not quite sure that I am not the greatest humbug that ever lived. Two minutes more. Do you bear in mind that Lady Kirkhope said she would call on me?"

"I will see to that. Am I forgiven for introducing you to her?"

Mona smiled. "I shall take my revenge by introducing you to a much greater woman, my friend Doris Colquhoun."

"When am I to meet you again? May I call?"

"No."

"How do you get home to-night?"

"Miss Bonthron sends me in a cab."

"Shall you be at the ball ?"

"No."

"You can easily get a good chaperon."

"Oh yes."

"Will you go to the ball if I ask it as a personal favour to me ? "

Mona reflected. "I don't see why I should not," she said, simply.

"Thank you. And in the meantime, Miss Maclean, don't be in too great a hurry to stand or fall with anybody. You have not only yourself to think of, you know; we are all members one of another. And now behold your prey ! Take me to your stall, and I will buy whatever you like."

The Sahib was not the only victim who yielded himself up unreservedly to Mona's tender mercies that day. Mr Brown came to the bazaar in the afternoon with a five-pound note in his pocket, and something more than four pound ten was spent at Miss Bonthron's stall.

CHAPTER XXXIX.

THE BALL.

A SPACIOUS hall with a well-waxed floor; a pro-
fusion of coloured lights and hothouse plants; a
small string-band capable of posing any healthy,
human thing under twenty-three with the reiterated query, " Where are the joys like dancing ? "
—all these things may be had on occasion, even
in an old-world fishing town on the bleak east
coast.

For youth is youth, thank heaven ! over all
the great wide world ; and the sturdy sonsy
northern girl, in her spreading gauzy folds of
white or blue, is as desirable in the eyes of
the shy young clerk, in unaccustomed swallow-
tails, as is the languid, dark-eyed daughter
of the South to her picturesque impassioned
lover. Nay, the awkward sheepish youth himself, he too is young, and, for some blue-eyed

girl, his voice may have the irresistible cadence, his touch the magnetic thrill, that Romeo's had for Juliet.

So do not, I pray you, despise my provincial ball, because the dancing falls short alike in the grace of constant habit and in the charm of absolute *naïveté*. The room is all aglow with youth and life and excitement. One must be a cynic indeed not to take pleasure in that. There is something beautiful too, surely, even in the proud self-consciousness with which the " Provost's lady " steps out to head the first quadrille with good Sir Roderick, and in the shy delight with which portly dames, at the bidding of grey-haired sires, forget the burden of years, and renew the days of their youth.

At Doris's earnest request, Mona had come to the ball with her party, for of course the Bonthrons disapproved of the whole proceeding. Rachel had insisted on going to the bazaar on the last day, to see the show and pick up a few bargains ; and, as the hall was overheated, and nothing would induce her to remove her magnificent fur-lined cloak, she had caught more cold on returning to the open air. Mona had offered very cordially to stay at home with her

on the night of the ball; but Rachel had been
sufficiently ill to read two sermons in the course
of the day; and, in the fit of magnanimity
naturally consequent on such occupation, she
had stoutly and kindly refused to listen to a
proposal which seemed to her more generous
than it really was.

It was after ten when the party from the
Towers entered the brilliant, resounding, whirl-
ing room. The Sahib had half expected that
Lady Kirkhope, in her pursuit of a "lark,"
would accompany them; but she "drew the
line," she said, "at dancing with the grocer," so
a few of the gentlemen went alone. There was
a good deal of amusement among them as they
drove down in the waggonette, on the subject
of the partners they might reasonably expect;
and it was with no small pride that the Sahib
introduced them to Doris and Mona.

Mona wore the gown in which Lucy had
said she looked like an empress. It was not
suitable for dancing, but she did not mean to
dance; and certainly she in her rich velvet,
and Doris in her shimmering silk, were a won-
drous contrast to most of the showily dressed
matrons and gauzy girls.

Doris as usual was very soon the quiet little centre of an admiring group; and even Mona, who had come solely to look on, and to enjoy a short chat with the Sahib, received an amount of attention that positively startled her when she thought of her " false position."

Of course she was pleased. It seemed like a fairy tale, that almost within a mile of the shop she should be received so naturally as a lady and a woman of the world; but, in point of fact, the Cooksons and Mrs Ewing were the only people who knew that she was Miss Simpson's assistant. Her regular *clientèle* was of too humble a class socially to be represented at the ball; her acquaintances in the neighbourhood were limited almost entirely to Rachel's friends and the members of the Baptist Chapel,—two sections of the community which were not at all likely to give support to such a festivity; and even people who had seen her repeatedly in her everyday surroundings, failed to recognise her in this handsome woman who had come to the ball with a very select party from St Rules.

Matilda glowed with triumph as she watched her friend move in a sphere altogether above her own ; she longed to proclaim to every one how she had known all the time that Miss Maclean was a princess in disguise. How aghast Clarinda would be at her own stupidity, and with what shame she would recall her pointless sarcasms—Clarinda, who that very evening had said, she at least gave the shop-girl the credit of believing that the lace was imitation and the pearls false

The night was wearing on, and Mona was sitting out a galop with Captain Steele, a handsome middle-aged man, whom the Sahib had introduced to her. They were conversing in a gay, frivolous strain, and Mona was reflecting how much easier it is to be entertaining in the evening if one has not been studying hard all day.

"Are you expecting any one?" asked the Captain, suddenly.

"No ; why do you ask ?"

"You look up so eagerly whenever a new arrival is ushered in."

"Do I ? It must be automatic. I scarcely know any one here."

But she coloured slightly as she spoke. His question made her conscious for the first time of

a wish away down in the depths of her heart—a
wish that Dr Dudley would come and see her
small success. He had seen her under such very
different conditions; he might arrive now any
day in Borrowness for the Christmas holidays;
why should he not be here to-night? It was
surely an innocent little wish as wishes go; but
on discovery it was treated ignominiously with
speedy and relentless eviction; and Mona gave
all the attention she could spare from the Captain's discourse to watching Doris and the
Sahib.

Poor little wish! Take a regret along with
you. You were futile and vain, for Dudley had
a sufficiently just estimate of his capabilities to
abstain at all times from dancing; and at that
moment, with fur cap over his eyes, he was
sleeping fitfully in the night express; and yet
perhaps you were a wise little wish, and how
different things might have been if you could
have been realised!

The wish was gone, however, and Mona was
watching her friends. A woman must be plain
indeed if she is not to look pretty in becoming
evening dress; and Doris, in her soft grey silk,
looked like a Christmas rose in the mists of

winter. She was talking brightly and eagerly, and the Sahib was listening with a smile that made his homely face altogether delightful. Mona wondered whether in all his honest life he had ever looked at any other woman with just that light in his eyes. "What a lucky man he will be who wins my Doris!" she said to herself; and close upon that thought came another. "They say matchmakers are apt to defeat their own ends, but if one praises the woman to the man, and abuses the man to the woman, one must at least be working in the right direction."

With a burst of harmony the band began a new waltz.

"Our dance, Miss Maclean," said the Sahib, coming up to her. "We are going to wander off to some far-away committee-room and swop confidences."

"It sounds nice, but my confidences are depressing."

"So are mine rather. Do you like this part of the world?"

"Do I like myself, in other words? Not much."

"Don't be philosophical. When all is said, there is nothing like gossip. I *don't* like this part of the world; in fact, I don't know myself in it; it is a fast, frivolous, imbecile world!"

"Socially speaking, I presume, not geographically. At least, those are not strictly the adjectives I should apply to my surroundings. How come you to be in such a world?"

"Oh, I met Kirkhope a few years ago. He was indulging in a fashionable run across India, and he ran up against me. I was able to put him up to a thing or two, and last month when I met him in Edinburgh, he invited me down. In a weak moment I accepted his invitation, and now you see Fortune has been kinder to me than I deserve."

"I saw you in Edinburgh as I went through one day," said Mona, and she told him she had been disappointed not to be able to speak to him at the station.

"How very disgusting!" he said. "Yes, Edinburgh is my home—my father's, at least."

"And had you never met Doris before I introduced you to her?"

The Sahib did not answer for a moment.

"I had not been introduced. I had seen her. Hers is not a face that one forgets."

"And yet it only gives a hint of all that lies

behind it. You might travel from Dan to Beersheba without finding such a gloriously unselfish woman, and such a perfect child of Nature."

"She is delightfully natural and unaffected. I think that is her great charm. What sort of man is Colquhoun? Of course every one knows him by name."

"Yes; he is very near the top of the tree in his profession. He is a scientist, too, but in that capacity he is a trifle—pathetic. Shall you call when you go back?"

"I have obtained permission to do so."

"You would do me a personal favour if you would enter into his scientific fads a little. Dear lovable old man! You will have to laugh in your sleeve pretty audibly before he suspects that you are doing it."

"I don't think I shall feel at all inclined to. Is Miss Colquhoun a scientist too?"

"She is something better. She loves a dog because it is a dog, a worm because it is a worm. Science must stand cap in hand before such genuine inborn love of Nature as hers."

Again there was a pause before the Sahib answered. Then he roused himself suddenly.

"It seems to me, Miss Maclean, that you are shirking your part of the bargain. I have confided to you how it is I come to be here. It is your innings now."

Mona sighed.

"When I last saw you, you were a burning and shining medical light. Wherefore the bushel?"

"That is right. Strike hard at the root of my *amour propre*. It is good for me, though I wince. I am here, Sahib, mainly because I failed twice in my Intermediate Medicine examination."

Another of the Sahib's characteristic pauses.

"How on earth did you contrive to do it?" he asked at last. "When one sees the duffers of men that pass——"

The colour on Mona's cheek deepened. "I don't think a very large proportion of duffers pass the London University medical examinations," she said. "Of course one makes excuses for one's self. One began hospital work too soon; one's knowledge was on a plane altogether above the level of the examination papers, &c. It is only in moments of rare and exceptional honesty that one says, as I

say to you now, 'I failed because I was a
duffer, and did not know my work.'"

"Nay, you don't catch me with chaff. That
is not the truth, and you don't think it is. I
don't call that honesty!"

But although the Sahib spoke harshly, his
heart was beating very warmly towards her
just then. He had always considered Mona
a clever and charming girl—a little too inde-
pendent, perhaps, but her habitual independ-
ence made it the more delightful to see her
submitting like a child to his questions, holding herself bound apparently for the moment
to answer honestly without fencing, however
much the effort might cost her.

"It is the truth, and nothing but the truth,"
she said. "I venture sometimes to think it is
not the whole truth."

"Shall you go in again?"

"Yes."

"When?"

"July."

"Do you think you will pass?"

"No."

"Then why do you do it?"

"I have promised."

Another long pause, and then it came un-
premeditatedly with a rush.

"Look here, Miss Maclean! chuck the whole
thing, and come back to India with me."

It was so absolutely unexpected, that for a
moment Mona thought it was a joke. "That
would be a delightfully simple way of cutting
the knot of the difficulty," she said gaily, but
before her sentence was finished she saw what
he meant. She tried not to see it, not to show
that she saw it, but the blood rushed over her
face and betrayed her.

"Do come," he said. "Will you? I never
cared for any woman as I care for you."

"Oh, Sahib," said Mona, "we cared for each
other, but not in that way. You have taught
me all I have missed in not having a brother."

She was not sorry for him; she was intensely annoyed at his stupidity. Not for a
moment did it occur to her that he might
really love her. He liked her, of course,
admired her, sympathised with her, at the
present moment pitied her; but did he really
suppose that a woman might not gladly accept
his friendship, admiration, sympathy, even his
pity, without wishing to have it all translated

into the vulgar tangible coin of an offer of
marriage? Was marriage for a woman, like
money for a beggar, the sole standard by which
all good feeling was to be tried?

She was not altogether at fault in her reading of his mind. The Sahib's sister Lena was
engaged to be married, and he had started on
his furlough with a vague general idea that if
he could fall in love and take a wife back with
him to India, it would be a very desirable
thing. Such an idea is as good a preventive
to falling in love as any that could be devised.

Among the girls he had met, Miss Maclean
was undoubtedly *facile princeps*. In many
respects she was cut out for the position; she
was one of those women who acquire a lighter
hand in conversation as they grow older, and
who go on mellowing to a rich matronly ma-
turity. In Anglo-Indian society she would be
something entirely new, and three months in
her own drawing-room would make a brilliant
woman of her.

During all the autumn months, while he
was shooting in Scotland, the Sahib had
delighted in the thought that he was deliberately keeping away from her, and had delighted

still more in the prospect of going "all by himself" to call upon her in London, to see whether the old impressions would be renewed in their full force. He had been bitterly angry and disappointed when he failed to find her at Gower Street, but the failure had gone very far to convince him that he really did love her.

And now had come this curious unexpected meeting at Kirkstoun. "Do you see that —person in the fur cloak?" Mona had said to him when he had dropped in for half an hour on the third day of the bazaar. "Don't be alarmed; I don't mean to introduce you; but that is my cousin. Now you know all that I can tell you." His momentary start and look of incredulity had not been lost upon her; but he had recovered himself in an instant, and had shown sufficient sense not to attempt any remark. And in truth, although he had been surprised and shocked, he had not been greatly distressed. "After all," he had said, "anybody could rake up a disreputable forty-second cousin from some ash-heap or other;" and the existence of such a person, together with Mona's breakdown in her medical career, gave him a pleasant, though unacknowledged,

sense of being the knight in the fairy tale
who is to deliver the captive princess from
all her woes. Moreover, Mona's peculiar circumstances had brought about an intimacy
between them that might otherwise have been
impossible. He had been admitted into one
of the less frequented chambers of her nature,
and he said to himself that it was a goodly
chamber. It was pleasant to see the colour
rise into her cheeks, to hear her breath come
quick while she talked to him; and to-night
—to-night she looked very beautiful, and no
shade of doubt was left on his mind that he
loved her.

"I suppose you are the best judge of
your feelings towards me," he said, coldly;
"but you will allow me to answer for mine."

The Sahib was a good man, and a simple-
hearted, but he knew his own value, and it
would have been strange if Mona's reply had
not surprised him. In fact he could only
account for it on one supposition, and that
supposition made him very angry and indig-
nant. His next words were natural, if un-
pardonable. Perhaps Mona's frankness was
spoiling him.

" Tell me," he said, sharply, " in the old Norway days, when we saw so much of each other,
was there some one else then ? "

Mona drew herself up. " I do call that
an insult," she said, quietly. " Do you suppose
that every unmarried woman is standing in
the market-place waiting for a husband ? Is
it impossible that a woman may prefer to
remain unmarried for the sake of all the work
in the world that only an unmarried woman
can do ? "

The Sahib's face brightened visibly for a
moment. Perhaps it was true, after all, that
this clever woman was more of a child in some
respects than half the flimsy damsels in the
ball-room.

" Miss Maclean," he said, " bear with my
dulness, and say to me these five words, ' There
is no one else.' "

Mona lifted her honest eyes.

" There is no one else," she said, simply.

" Thank you. Then if my sole rival is the
work that only an unmarried woman can do, I
decline to accept your answer."

" Don't be foolish, Mr Dickinson," said Mona,
gently. " You call me honest, and in this

respect I am absolutely honest. If there were the faintest shadow of a doubt in my mind I would tell you. There are very few people in the world whom I like and trust as I do you, but I would as soon think of marrying Sir Douglas Munro. And you — you are sacrificing yourself to your own chivalry. You want to marry me because you are sorry for me, because I have muddled my own life."

"That is not true. My one objection to you is that you are twice the man that I am."

Mona laughed. "*Eh bien! L'un n'empêche pas l'autre.* No, no ; you are much too good a man to be thrown away on a woman who only likes and trusts you."

"When do you leave this place?" he asked, doggedly.

"In March."

"And do you stop in Edinburgh on the way?"

"Yes ; I have promised to spend a week with the Colquhouns."

"Good. I will ask you then again."

"Dear Sahib," said Mona, earnestly, "I have not spoilt your life yet. Don't let

me begin to spoil it now. You cannot afford
to waste even three months over a chivalrous
fancy. Put me out of your mind altogether,
till you have married a bright young thing
full of enthusiasms, not a worn-out old cynic
like me. Then by-and-by, if she will let me be
her sister, you and I can be brother and sister
again."

"May I write to you during the next two
months ?"

"I think it would be a great mistake."

"Your will shall be law. But remember, I
shall be thinking of you constantly, and when
you are in Edinburgh I will come. Shall we go
back to the ball-room ?" He rose and offered
her his arm.

"Mr Dickinson, I absolutely refuse to leave
the question open. What is the use ?"

"You will not do even that for me ?"

"It would be returning evil for good."

"No matter. The results be on my own
head ! "

They were back in the noise and glare of the
ball-room, and further conversation was impossible.

"Who would have thought of meeting two charming *émancipées* down here?" said Captain Steele, as the men drove back to the Towers.

"If all *émancipées* are like Miss Colquhoun," said a young man with red hair and a retreating chin, "I will get a book and go round canvassing for women's rights to-morrow!"

END OF THE SECOND VOLUME.

PRINTED BY WILLIAM BLACKWOOD AND SONS.